Through the Storm

The Solar Storm Saga, Book One

By Kyle Pratt

CAMDEN CASCADE
PUBLISHING

Through the Storm
The Solar Storm Saga, Book One
By Kyle Pratt

Paperback ISBN: 978-0-9983756-4-9
First edition – September 25, 2017

Cover Design: Inspired Cover Designs

*   *   *

Sign up for my no-spam monthly newsletter and receive ***free*** ebooks, promotional offers, and discounts.

Details are at the end of the novel.

Acknowledgments

Creating a novel involves many people. Sure, I imagine the plot and write the manuscript, but as soon as I'm done, many more people become involved.

First of all, I need to thank my wife, Lorraine. She reads every chapter multiple times before anyone else sees it. Without her support, ideas, and constant encouragement, I would not be an author.

After Lorraine, the next to see any chapters are members of my critique groups. These include Robert Hansen, Barbara Blakey, Carolyn Bickel, Debby Lee, Kristie Kandoll, Pat Thompson, and LeeAnn Thompson. These people are more than fellow writers; they are friends and mentors.

After the critique group finishes with the manuscript, a few dedicated beta-readers pore over the novel. For this book, the beta-readers were William Childress, Micheal Hurley, Jennifer Vandenberg, and Debbie Majoros. These detail-orientated readers look for problems in grammar, plotting, and continuity.

Thank you all for making this book possible.

Prologue: Events on the Sun

Six storms churned on the sun. Over several weeks they grew to encompass an area fifteen times the size of Earth. Invisible magnetic lines of force danced, curved, and weaved above and between them. But on this particular day, as the magnetic fields bent and reconnected, a huge amount of ionized gas, called plasma, became trapped in the sun's atmosphere.

For the next few days, the plasma swirled and pitched in the corona region of the atmosphere, while it absorbed radiant energy and grew hotter than a nuclear fireball.

Finally, the superheated mass reached a temperature of more than ten million degrees Celsius and exploded as a solar flare. Much of it fell back to the sun but, on the edge of the magnetic fields, several planet-sized clouds snapped like a whip, broke free of the sun's gravity, and flung into space.

Astronomers call these plasma clouds Coronal Mass Ejections, or CMEs. Each possessed more energy than an entire year of the world's electrical production; these were hurtled at speeds faster than a bolt of lightning on a collision course with Earth.

Day zero

Reno, Nevada, Saturday, September 3rd

The world might end tonight and the last words Neal Evans had spoken to his oldest son were in anger.

No, don't be paranoid. Everything will probably be fine. But just to be sure, Neal hunted for the TV remote. When he finally located it in the chair where he had left it, he switched to a trustworthy news channel. There, talking heads discussed upcoming Senate hearings on a new crime-fighting bill.

Such mundane stories rarely held his interest. Neal retrieved the toiletries bag from his luggage. Before heading to the shower, he turned up the TV volume so he could listen to the news.

Several people at the conference had talked about the aurora borealis being visible tonight. In the hotel lobby, a young man spoke with others about an electromagnetic pulse that could end civilization.

Neal glanced out the window. The sun drifted low in the sky, barely above the big box store across the street. He wasn't that paranoid. Chances were that no aurora would light the sky tonight, and almost certainly no EMP would slam civilization to its knees. Well, at least not before he returned home tomorrow.

He undressed and enjoyed the cool spray of the shower for a moment. Then he lathered head to toe, a habit from his navy days.

It had been a long seven-hour drive from Vegas to Reno, and he didn't want to worry, pace, or even think. He wanted only this cool shower and a mind-numbing action movie. He would start home to Washington state early on Sunday and arrive there in the afternoon.

As he rinsed the soap from his body, the dong of a news alert sounded.

"We have additional information about the lead story of the day. The National Oceanic and Atmospheric Administration, along with the Space Weather Prediction Center, reported earlier in the day that a coronal mass ejection had occurred on the sun."

Neal turned off the shower, stepped onto the cold tiled floor, and grabbed a towel.

"We have Dr. Jacob Becker on the phone. He's a professor of astronomy at Stanford. Doctor, what is a coronal mass ejection?"

"These are huge bursts of gas and electromagnetic radiation thrown off by the sun. They travel through space like clouds but at speeds of up to thousands of kilometers per second."

"Yeah, I know all of this," Neal grumbled. He hung the towel over one shoulder as he walked from the bathroom. "Where is the plasma headed?" he asked the television.

"Should we be concerned about this one?" the announcer asked.

"Usually, no. However, this is an extraordinarily large CME, on the G4 or G5 scale, and it is on course to hit the Earth's magnetic field."

Neal rubbed his chin. Local Washington state media often turned minor floods into biblical deluges, or two inches of snow into the storm of the decade, giving Seattle residents an excuse to stay home. The CME might be headed toward Earth, but was it large enough to do more than dance across the sky as northern lights? He continued to listen.

"FEMA advises that due to the scale of this phenomenon, there is a likelihood of some power and communications failures."

The government might consider the loss of phones, Internet, and power for a day or two to be catastrophic, but Neal would be fine without them.

"… of this, federal and state officials are urging people to stay home and avoid travel tonight."

"Stay home and watch the aurora," the announcer advised with a practiced smile.

Neal lowered the television volume to a normal level and booted his computer. As a backyard and warm weather astronomer, he knew where to find answers. When the browser filled the screen, Neal logged into his favorite astronomy forum. There, a dozen professionals discussed the solar storm that hurtled toward the planet.

Most scientists on the forum argued the storm would be no worse than G4; a few others warned of a G5 occurrence. One scientist, Arthur Blake, compared it to the Carrington Event of 1859.

"That solar storm created aurora around the world, as far south as the Caribbean," Blake had typed on the forum page. "But it also caused sparks and shocks along the telegraph system. What will this do to modern electronic technology?"

While the size of the storm remained under debate by the astronomers, the course and speed had been calculated. It would hit the Earth's magnetosphere in ten hours.

The talking heads on TV were still predicting limited power and communications outages and advising to wait it out at home. If this was their typical overreaction, he had nothing to worry about, and might even enjoy the aurora. However, if this was a Carrington Event, power and communications might fail across huge parts of the planet. Other systems, even cars, might fail. Neal grabbed his phone and tapped the number for home.

He heard only a busy signal.

He called his older son's cell phone, but the call forwarded to his voice mail. Again he remembered their argument before he had left home Thursday afternoon. Conner had wanted to go hunting over the weekend. Neal had insisted he stay home and keep an eye on Drake.

"Why do I have to babysit while you go to Vegas?" Conner's face grew redder with each word.

"I'm your father and I need you to do this—so do it." Neal had stormed from the house.

Again he tried both numbers and received the same unwanted results. With a flick of the hand, he tossed the phone onto the bed.

Within hours, modern civilization might be shaken to its core. *No, don't overreact. Tonight will probably be a minor footnote in history.*

As he continued to watch the news and monitor the online forum, he evaluated what he knew for certain. The CME was large and would hit Earth in ten hours. Those were all the available facts.

Using the computer, Neal plotted his route home. The quickest way would take just under ten hours. Should he drive all night? More than one friend had accused him of being paranoid, but what he knew concerned him.

When the final meeting of the financial planning conference in Las Vegas ended, Neal had reluctantly prepared to drive home. He had little reason to hurry. Since Beth had died, home had been a place of tension. His two teenage sons seemed distant, even cool. How could he bridge such a gap?

Beth had always been his guide to raising the boys. She had been the outgoing, loving, and empathetic one. He had been the breadwinner. Those traditional roles had worked for them. When they went out, she smiled and talked. He tried to grin and did a lot of listening. Neal often joked that he was her stoic bodyguard.

Then, in a flash, she had died, leaving him alone. He should have been there. He should have protected her.

Since he wasn't eager to return home, a place of so many memories, heartache, and tension, he had planned to visit an old navy buddy on his way back. He shook his head. It would be best to be home, near his sons, and sleep in the bed he had shared with Beth. He pushed the heartache from his thoughts.

A check of airline schedules revealed a long list of canceled flights. Neal leaned back in the chair. How serious is this situation? He checked the rail schedule. No trains left for Portland or Seattle in the next two days. Perhaps driving was the best option. If nothing terrible happened, he would arrive home tired but with his car. He tried to phone his boys again but with no success.

A glance at a clock showed just past seven. There would be no rest for him tonight, and he would need copious amounts of coffee for the trip home.

Neal packed his bags and tossed them into the trunk. Then, he pawed through the old rucksack that housed his bug-out supplies: water bottles, basic tools, small camp stove, P-38 can opener, matches, emergency radio, tarp, first aid kit, and more. He inspected more for reassurance than to inventory items. When he felt the pistol, he stopped.

Neal removed the Sig P250 and placed it in an inside pocket of his jacket, along with some ammo. He checked out of the hotel, drove to the nearest ATM, where he withdrew five hundred dollars in twenty-dollar bills, and then filled his thermos with coffee from a nearby kiosk.

Amply caffeinated, Neal drove north on Highway 395 out of Reno. With each mile, the electric lights of civilization gave way to the darkness of night. However, this was only the natural transition from urban Reno to rural Northern California. He wondered if he would even know the moment when the CME hit the Earth.

For nearly two hours he drove north, sipping coffee and switching between satellite and local radio stations. Eight hours remained before the event, and he had learned little more.

The darkness hid the surrounding countryside, but Neal knew the route along the secondary highways, through the dry scrub brush, scattered pine, and wildflower landscape.

South of Susanville, Highway 395 veered east, but Neal continued straight into town. Spotting a small roadside diner, he pulled into the nearly empty parking lot, walked inside, and stopped at the counter.

A gum-chewing waitress in her early thirties rang up a customer and then turned to Neal with a smile. "How can I help you?"

"Could you fill my thermos with coffee?"

"Sure." She retrieved a pot. "I'm guessing you don't want decaf."

"No." Neal shook his head. "I'll be driving all night."

"Where're you headed?" She twisted on the lid.

"Washington state."

"Really?" Her eyes widened. "Are you driving that far because of the sun storm thing?"

He nodded.

She giggled. "I'm thinking this is a bunch of hype like Y2K. Do you think anything will actually happen?"

Embarrassed by his worries, Neal shrugged. "I've got two boys in Washington state. I want to be home or close to it anyway." After paying her, he stepped away and then stopped. "Where is the nearest gas station?"

She pointed. "Just down the road. Good luck. I hope you make it home safe."

"Thanks." Neal's gut churned. Too much coffee on an empty stomach, or was it worry about the end of the world? He would eat at his next stop.

Cars idled in line from the gas station pumps back onto the road. It seemed like a town meeting with people out of their cars as they talked and argued while waiting in line to top off their gas tanks.

Should he leave or get in line? He let out a frustrated sigh and pulled in behind the last car. As he waited, he checked his watch, recalculated the drive for the fifteenth time, and tried to call home and Conner's cell. Why couldn't he reach his sons? He set the alarm on his phone for one minute before the predicted arrival of the CME.

Over the next fifteen minutes, he edged forward until his car pulled to the pump. Minutes later he continued on his way with a full tank of gasoline, a hot thermos of coffee, and high spirits. He had even filled the gas can in the trunk.

Traffic continued to be light and he remained ahead of schedule. He would be home before the CME slammed the Earth. Not wanting to be pulled over by the police, Neal struggled to reduce his speed to the posted limit, or just a little above. As he neared the town of Adin, flashing red-and-blue lights ahead caught his attention.

A state patrol vehicle blocked the way.

Neal checked his GPS and determined that the wide spot in the road must be Jupiter Junction. He had passed through it going to the conference but had taken little notice. On the right stood a small motel, and then his lights caught a strange teepee-like structure on the left. He thought the giant badminton birdie was actually some sort of industrial burner, but he didn't have the time or inclination to investigate. Whatever the thing was, he knew of only one along the route so easily determined his exact location.

Two officers stood on opposite sides of the road just beyond the junction with Highway 299.

Neal tapped his brakes to slow the car.

One officer approached as he pulled to a stop. "We're encouraging people to stay home tonight. Where are you headed?"

"Home. Washington state." Immediately Neal wished he had said Adin, a small town just up the road, but the Washington plates on the car would have made that a tough sell.

"I'm pleased you're headed home, but there's been an accident up ahead. A tanker truck and car hit head-on. The highway is closed to all but local traffic." The officer pointed to Highway 299 that disappeared into the darkness to the west. "Probably best that you keep to the main roads tonight anyway."

"Why?" Neal asked, although he knew the reason.

"Perhaps you've heard about the storm on the sun. If it causes electrical and communication problems, it might be best to be near other people."

Neal thought the opposite might be true but nodded to the officer as he tapped the information into his GPS. "That'll reroute me southwest—over a hundred miles."

"But then you can get on the interstate and shoot straight north. This road is going to be closed for hours. If the sun storm causes car problems, like some are saying, help can find you much easier along the freeway."

If his car failed when the CME hit, Neal wondered why the highway patrol thought their vehicles would be spared. He stared longingly down the deserted highway ahead. If civilization crashed back to a pre-industrial era tonight, he would have preferred to be on a quiet backcountry road. However, the officer didn't seem inclined to let him pass. If he hurried, sped, he might at least be near home before the solar storm hit.

Neal headed down the directed road. After several moments he glanced at his watch. Less than six hours until … he didn't know, and that scared him.

* * *

Even though traffic had remained light, and he had made good time, Neal's gut churned with anxiety. In the city of Redding, he merged onto Interstate 5 and pressed the gas pedal. Now five hours into his trip, how long would it take to reach home? A few taps on the GPS screen revealed still more than seven hours of driving ahead. He glanced at his watch; less than four hours remained until the CME would hit Earth.

Neal chugged coffee, turned up the radio, and tried to gain time as he sped north. For many minutes, he was distracted as he listened to the all-night conspiracy program on the radio.

"This is the vanguard of an alien invasion," a caller named Doyle proclaimed. "They want to destroy our technology and let millions of us die. Then they'll come in and mop up the survivors."

A few argued that the CME was natural, but most thought aliens, the government, communists, or terrorists were somehow involved.

Neal shook his head. "And people call me paranoid." He laughed and sipped more coffee. As the miles rolled by, his mind drifted from the radio, to what might happen, and then to the need to reach home. The hills rolled, and the highway weaved, making it more difficult to maintain a steady speed, but when he could, he let his speedometer edge up. He raced down a hill and around a curve.

As the highway straightened, the familiar red and blue lights flashed behind him.

He removed his foot from the pedal, glanced at the speedometer, and cursed as the numbers slid to ten miles over the speed limit. He prayed the patrol car would pass him.

It didn't.

He steered the car to the side of the highway and stopped.

"License and registration please."

He handed them over.

The officer examined the documents. "Why were you going so fast, Mr. Evans?"

"I'm trying to get home to my family before … before whatever happens."

The officer nodded. "I understand," He handed the documents back to Neal. "You won't get home by driving carelessly."

Actually millions of careless drivers got home safely every day. But he only uttered, "Yes, officer."

"I won't give you a ticket this time, but slow down." The patrolman touched his hat and returned to his car.

Neal pulled back onto the freeway and gradually increased his speed to the limit and set the cruise control.

As the night waned, he crossed into Oregon. A glance at his watch showed that in less than two hours the world as he knew it might cease to exist, yet he remained five hours from home.

Time flew as he hurried through Medford and Grants Pass.

Minutes later the alarm on his phone beeped. He glanced at his watch and held his breath. Seconds later, red, green, yellow and purple curtains of light danced out of the north and weaved back and forth across the sky. The radio hissed, popped and fell into silence. His phone alarm died mid-tone.

Along a lonely stretch of Interstate 5, Neal's car coughed, sputtered, and rolled to a stop.

Day one

Rural Lewis County, Washington, Sunday, September 4th

Drake Evans rolled over in bed. The room seemed unusually bright, but the alarm hadn't gone off. The rooster crowed and one of the goats bleated. He pulled the covers over his head. The animals needed feeding, but why get up early?

With his brother on an overnight hunting trip, and Dad at a conference, he had been able to do what he wanted—for the first time in his almost sixteen years. It might not yet be his birthday, but last night sure felt like it.

When his older brother, Conner, said he might go hunting, Drake encouraged him. "I'm plenty old enough to spend a couple of days by myself."

Friday evening, Conner had packed his gear and admonished his brother to be responsible. "Remember to feed the animals and no parties."

Drake had waved goodbye to his older brother, dashed into the house, and invited six friends over for some Saturday evening revelry. All of them had shown up, even Ashley.

Drake smiled as he recalled the evening of pizza, movies, video games, and Ashley with her long blonde hair, tight jeans, and green blouse that seemed to curve around all her shapeliness. Unfortunately, she stayed only two hours, saying that her parents would expect her home when they returned from their "date night." She made an "ick" face as she said it. Drake thought it looked cute on her.

His other friends stayed hours longer and he thought the evening ended well. If high school started like this, it should be a fun four years.

Of course, after he fed the animals he would need to clean the house. Drake had no desire for Dad to return and see the mess left from last night. He lifted his head from the pillow to check the time. Where soft red numbers should have glowed, only black appeared.

"Huh?" He sat on the side of the bed. Morning sunlight illuminated the room. Rubbing his eyes, he climbed from bed and flicked the nearest light switch to test for power.

Nothing.

He threw the switch up and down, but no light shined forth. The electricity was out.

* * *

Rural Chelan County, Washington, Sunday, September 4th

Conner Evans gazed into the late morning sky but couldn't see the smoke that irritated his nose. He enjoyed the smell of flora and fauna, tinged with mushrooms, mold, and even damp earth and rotting wood. But this was the acrid odor of manmade materials—tires and plastic. The smell worried him as he descended the trail toward civilization. Few things out here would cause such odors, except his burning truck.

He sped down the trail toward the gravel parking lot less than a mile ahead.

This trip hadn't been a total bust. Although the prize deer he spotted earlier in the year remained elusive, a weekend alone in the forest had refreshed him, and before dawn, he had awakened to a sky painted by God. Waves of green, yellow, and reds danced across a black background. Cross "See an aurora" off the bucket list.

Conner shifted the backpack and rifle on his shoulders and jogged on. With each step he uttered a prayer that his vehicle was okay. He shook his head. Why would it burn? There hadn't been a forest fire. Conner looked about. Nope, no trees burned, and he hadn't seen another person all weekend. Still, people did travel out this way. The parking lot lay less than a hundred yards from a small lake.

Ahead, a deer and her yearling scurried across the path, their hooves tapping and clicking on the stones.

Would anyone else be at the lake? He glanced at his wrist out of habit but had left his watch and phone in his backpack, and he had no intention of stopping and digging either out now.

This was the Sunday before Labor Day. He rubbed his chin. Even a site this far out would attract a few people to fish and camp, but they wouldn't harm his vehicle. Would they?

Conner ran the last hundred yards and bounded breathlessly into the parking area. There, alone in the lot, sat his apparently unharmed red pickup. Feeling a bit silly, he slowed and walked to the truck. Close up it still looked fine. The odor hadn't grown stronger as he approached his truck but still hung in the air.

Just to be sure, he stepped around it and even looked underneath for any hint of burning.

With a sigh, he unlocked the door, hoisted his pack into the back of the cab, and set his rifle behind it. Then he slid into the driver's seat and turned the key.

The usual dash lights flickered, but the engine didn't budge—not even a sound.

He tried again.

Nothing.

Conner banged the steering wheel, prayed, and turned the key.

"Nada."

He looked around the dirt lot. Even on this three-day weekend, no one else had driven up here.

"Just my lousy luck." Conner retrieved the cellphone from his backpack. No service—of course. Then, as he stared at the phone, it died. "Oh, this day just keeps getting better!" He shoved it in a pocket. A ten-mile hike awaited him before a cell tower would be in range—if his phone would turn on.

He imagined walking the two hundred miles back home. He shook his head. *No, that's ridiculous.* His luck was bound to change. Someone would come along and give him a ride. He needed only to trek somewhere so he could call the auto club or find a ride back to civilization. Either way, someone would fix the truck. Still, he might have to walk the twenty miles to the freeway. He looked under the hood. All the belts were good. He tightened the battery connections. Then he tried to start the vehicle again, without success.

Conner considered what to do with his rifle. Bringing it would reduce his chances of getting a ride, but leaving it in the truck didn't seem like a good idea. He looked into the sky at a sun already past its zenith. He might need to camp along the road. Like a Boy Scout leader, his dad had always preached being prepared, and in this case, it was probably a good idea. The food, water, and sleeping bag would make camping, even for one night, more agreeable.

As he walked away from his truck, he sniffed the air and wondered again what caused the pungent smoke.

The road he walked along hugged one side of a small river valley. Trees lined the right side of the road, with few on the left that sloped toward the river. He scanned the ridge of hills to the south and then lifted his gaze higher into the sky. The temperature remained pleasant despite the bright sun. A hawk drifted on the air currents high above.

His spirits revived a bit as he hiked. Maybe everything would work out. Then he remembered his father would be home sometime today. Conner had planned to talk with his dad about enlisting in the marines, instead of attending college. Conner was supposed to be watching over his little brother, and for any talk about the marines to be successful, he would need to arrive home before his father.

He hoped Drake hadn't burned down the farm. Conner didn't think he had reason to worry, but still he hurried.

A few hundred yards farther along the road, the stench of burning rubber and plastic grew stronger. He strode around a sharp bend in the road.

Billows of smoke told him he had found the source of the smell before he actually spotted the smoldering wreck. Skid marks showed where the driver of the silver-gray SUV had tried to stop but plunged off the road, rolled down the slope, and slammed into a tree. The impact left the car wrapped like a "C" around a large Douglas fir.

Conner shook his head. The awful smoke and charred metal of the wreck stood in sharp contrast to the nearby forest and stream. He hoped the occupants were okay and had left. Without a thought, he gulped air and then gagged on the acrid fumes. Before continuing his journey, he had to be certain no one remained inside.

Taking shallow breaths, he hiked down the slope. "Hello? Is anyone there? Do you need help?"

No one answered, giving him hope that the occupants had survived and left.

With tentative steps, he approached the vehicle.

Windows were shattered and tires still smoked, leaving only charred rubble within the SUV.. Thankfully, he spotted nothing that looked like a body.

Then he noticed a tarp neatly spread out five yards from the wreck with stones holding down the corners.

Conner stepped closer, and then stopped, unwilling to see what might lie beneath, but he had to know. If he wanted to be a marine, he couldn't succumb to the fear that grew within him.

He knelt and slowly folded back the cover. The day got worse.

* * *

Rural Josephine County, Oregon, Saturday, September 4th

Small red symbols lit the dash. Neal turned the key and heard a click and then nothing. He opened the car door and the overhead light shone. He lifted the hood and another light illuminated the engine.

It might be a coincidence that the aurora had splashed across the sky at the moment his vehicle had died. No, as strange as it sounded, a storm on the sun burning out most modern electronics, like those in his car, might be the answer. He shook his head. Despite all he had read, the thought of it still seemed bizarre.

He looked north and south along the highway but couldn't see or hear another vehicle. Soon people would be hiking along the freeway looking for food and safety, but now only the breeze rustled in his ears. It might be safer to be alone, but he needed to be home, and that meant moving. He tapped the Sig P250 in the holster compartment of his vest. *I sure hope I don't need it.*

Neal strode to the back of his vehicle, opened the toolbox, and pulled out two crescent wrenches. This was at least worth a try.

He had read somewhere that during an electromagnetic pulse, a latch-up, or short circuit, could occur in car electronics. One way to correct the problem was to momentarily disconnect one of the battery cables. He returned to the front of the car. That would reboot the systems and allow the vehicle to restart. He hoped.

Staring at the two battery cables, he couldn't recall which needed to be removed, so he removed both and cleaned the posts with a rag. He shook his head. Why clean them? The car wasn't going to start.

Another glance along the freeway revealed no vehicles or people within sight. Alone on this forested section of highway, he felt like the only person left on Earth. He reattached the cables, slid into the car, and turned the key. The roar of the engine surprised him. Thrilled, he dropped both wrenches on the passenger seat and hurried north.

* * *

Rural Chelan County, Washington, Sunday, September 4th

Beneath the tarp, a mother and child lay beside each other. The deep cuts, compound fractures, and burns told Conner what he needed to know. They were dead.

He gagged at the sight, stumbled back, and turned away, but the image of the mangled woman and child remained fixed in his mind. He coughed and spat. After several moments, he pulled the tarp back over the bodies, being careful not to look at them.

He climbed to the road, wondering what to do. As he reached the pavement, his thoughts coalesced into a plan. Someone, probably the husband and father, had placed the bodies under the covering. If he had gone to the parking lot at the lake, Conner would have seen him. So, he must be hiking back toward the town in search of help. Conner hurried to catch up with the unfortunate man and give what aid and comfort he could.

As he trotted, Conner listened, gazed along the river to his left and into the trees on his right. He spotted a few deer and a bald eagle but no other humans. Eventually, he slowed his pace and thought about the morning's events. The idea that the only two cars in this rural area were both out of commission seemed extraordinary. Also, this was a holiday weekend. There should be some traffic.

He stopped and listened. No hint of a car engine in the distance. No plane flew overhead, only a hawk using an updraft to soar. Often he had been alone in the forest, but it had always been a good feeling. More like solitude than alone. He wouldn't admit it to anyone, but this isolation made his skin crawl.

Minutes later, Conner spotted a dark smear on bramble leaves beside the road. With one finger he touched it. *Sticky and red. Blood?* He wiped the finger on his pants.

Several yards beyond, he noticed a similar smear on dirt along the edge of the pavement. At a run, he rounded the next bend. Ahead, someone lay unmoving on the gravel shoulder. "Hey, are you okay?"

He rushed forward and knelt beside a man just a bit older than himself but about the same weight, stocky build, and similar brown hair. The blood stains on his shirt and pants seemed to confirm he had been in the wreck.

Conner rolled him onto his back.

Blank expressionless eyes stared into the sky. Conner touched the body, already cool to the touch, but still checked for a pulse. He found none.

Are you the husband and father? Did your wife and child die up the road? Were you going for help? Conner wondered if the entire family had died due to one tragic accident. Such thoughts, the blood, and the blank eyes overwhelmed him. He fell backward onto his rear as bile climbed in his throat.

* * *

Rural Josephine County, Oregon, Sunday, September 4th

As he drove, Neal pulled out his phone, dialed, and prayed that his sons were safe.

Nothing happened.

He stared at it in anger. No bars filled the corner of his screen.

He corrected his drift toward the center of the highway and dropped the phone on the passenger seat with the wrenches. He glanced around for cell towers. Surely some were within range, but had they survived the events of last night?

Neal recalled that just before the solar storm strike, the GPS advised that he had five hours remaining on his drive, so he still had more than four hours of worry ahead of him.

He tapped the device to turn it on. The display appeared, but it showed an endless search for his location. Neal wondered if the device had been damaged by the solar storm or whether the satellites had been destroyed. Perhaps both. He left it on, hoping that it might function at some point. If needed, he still had paper maps in the glovebox.

Wanting to hear another human voice, Neal turned on the radio. Static crackled from the speaker. The pre-sets had been lost when he disconnected the battery, so he had it search. As he drove along it looped through the AM dial without pause. He tried the satellite radio with no success.

As he rounded a gentle bend he spotted three vehicles on the road. A sedan sat on the highway shoulder a hundred yards ahead. Two other vehicles stood motionless in the road a quarter mile beyond. Neal wanted to speed by them, but he felt some obligation to stop and assist. The hood stood open on the nearest car. Jaw clenched, Neal slowed as he drew near.

Inside, a woman about Neal's age fiddled with a cell phone. A man with thin graying hair stared over the engine. As Neal pulled to a stop in front of the disabled auto, the man stood erect and kept a wary eye on him.

Neal tapped the pistol in his vest. *Don't be paranoid.* He forced a smile, grabbed the crescent wrenches from the car seat, and stepped out.

The man looked him up and down.

Neal took a few cautious steps. "If your car won't start, it's probably because of the CME."

The man cast him a confused glance.

"The storm on the sun." Neal held up the tools. "I might be able to start it."

"I wondered if that was why all the cars stopped." The man nodded toward the other two vehicles. "That's probably why my wife can't call the auto club."

Neal smiled. "Yeah, no tow trucks today." He shook the man's hand and introduced himself.

"My name is Chris Bowman. That's my wife, Ellie."

She waved from the passenger seat and continued to tap on her phone.

Chris shook his head. "I wish she'd give up trying to call our kids."

Neal grinned at the man's frustration, and then explained why the car stopped and what he would be doing. He pulled the first battery cable loose.

"Is this how you got your car going?"

Neal nodded. "And hopefully your car will be next."

As Neal continued to work, Chris talked. "We flew down to San Francisco to visit friends. I didn't think much about the storm on the sun thing until they announced that all the flights that night were canceled. Then the wife wanted to leave. I borrowed this car and headed north. Ellie wanted to be near family in Portland, but well ...." He shrugged. "We didn't make it."

Neal reconnected both cables. "You still might. Get in and try to start it."

Chris slid behind the wheel and turned the key.

The car roared.

Neal shut the hood with a thud.

Chris and Ellie smiled at him.

Neal dropped the wrenches into his car and smiled back. Helping others felt good.

Chris leaned out the window. "Thanks." His eyes focused farther down the highway and then widened in fear.

Neal turned. Only fifty yards away, three men ran toward him. The lead man's long gray hair bounced as he ran. He wore a faded T-shirt and jeans, but Neal's eyes shifted from the man's scruffy appearance to the pistol in his hand.

As he stepped toward his vehicle, Neal drew his own weapon.

The three slowed to a walk, formed a line before Neal, and continued to edge closer. The two on either side of the scruffy old guy were younger and wore somewhat better clothes but could have been sons.

Scruffy held up his free hand. "We just need help with our cars."

"Do you usually ask favors with a gun in your hand?"

"You have one. I need to protect myself."

Neal had no interest in arguing about who had drawn first. "Back up and we can talk."

"All I want to know is why your car is running, and how you got this one to go."

"Disconnect the battery cables for a few seconds and reconnect them." *But in your case, I hope it doesn't work.*

Scruffy cast Neal an incredulous look. "You expect me to believe that? Show me on our cars."

Chris nodded from his running vehicle. "That's all he did and it worked."

Scruffy stepped forward. "You put the gun down and show me exactly how you did it."

Neal shook his head. "I think you can figure it out."

Scruffy inched forward.

Stepping backward, Neal adjusted his aim. "Don't come any closer."

"You won't shoot. You're not the type." Scruffy laughed and jumped forward.

A gun fired.

* * *

Rural Lewis County, Washington, Sunday, September 4th

Drake's family had lived on the farm for most of his life, and in all that time the animals were fed before he ate. His mother had usually cooked breakfast while he and his brother took care of chores. After she died, Dad regularly prepared the meal, although it often consisted of just cold cereal or oatmeal. Cooked breakfasts were a rare treat, usually made by Dad or Conner. For reasons he seldom concerned himself with, Drake had never been asked to cook any meal. He yawned and stretched. His breakfast would come first this morning.

Gruff, their Labrador retriever, hurried to Drake's side the moment he opened the bedroom door. "Yeah, we'll get breakfast soon." Drake used the bathroom and drank water. The flow from the faucet seemed weak, but he took little notice.

Moving on to the living room, he tapped the remote to turn on the TV. Still tired from the party, he yawned and looked about. The couch had been pulled up close to the television for video game playing. Paper plates lay scattered on the floor, along with bits of chips, dip, and popcorn. Several glasses sat half full on tables. He didn't look forward to a day of housework.

When the television remained black, he recalled the power outage. *What do you do when the power is off? Should I call the electric company? What's their number?*

They owned a generator, but he decided not to use it. The power would certainly be back on soon.

Drake retrieved the phone handset from the floor and returned it to the receiver. He hoped no one had tried to call him. He didn't want his dad, or even Conner, asking too many questions about the weekend.

Stomach grumbles pushed Drake toward the kitchen as memories of the party flitted through his mind. Ashley nearly beat him at two video games. She played well but seemed more interested in talking. He prayed that the opportunity for another party would soon occur.

Drake grabbed milk from a dark fridge and cereal from the pantry.

Gruff whined.

"Okay," Drake said. "I'll feed you first, but the livestock can wait."

Gruff gulped his food as Drake poured milk on his cereal.

He had expected quiet in the powerless house but, even with the kitchen window open, heard no rumble of cars, chainsaws, lawnmowers, or planes outside. He crunched more cereal and then picked up the spoon and bowl, walked to the French doors, and stepped onto the back porch. From here he could see much of the river valley and, through a gap in the trees, glimpse the freeway two miles away. On a typical day he could hear traffic but not this morning.

It's a holiday weekend and the power is out. Maybe everyone slept in.

Afterward, he added the bowl and spoon to a sink full of dirty dishes.

Feed the animals, clean the house, and wash dishes. That thought brought a sigh. He put on his shoes and headed outside with Gruff.

From inside the barn, he grabbed a bucket to fill with water for the animals. He stepped out and turned the spigot. No water gushed forth, only gurgling.

No electricity. He sighed. *No power for the well.* Beside the well house, his father had installed a hand pump, right out of a western movie. Drake considered using it to fetch the water he needed for the day.

"Gruff, come." He wanted to phone the power company before hand-pumping gallons of water.

Gruff growled as four horses ran into the barnyard.

Horses? Where did they come from? Drake grabbed the dog's collar. They had chickens, rabbits, a couple of pigs and goats but no horses. Then he remembered that the neighbors used an electric fence to keep theirs in. He shook his head. "This day isn't going to be any fun at all."

* * *

Rural Josephine County, Oregon, Sunday, September 4th

It took a second for Neal to realize that his gun had fired. He stared at it in his hand.

Scruffy moaned on the pavement.

One of the sons ran to the father's side and pulled up the bloody shirt. "Dad, are you …?" He pointed with a bloodstained hand at Neal. "You shot our dad."

"Where's Dad's gun?" the other son asked.

Tires squealed as Chris's vehicle lunged forward and passed between Neal and the others with only inches to spare.

Neal stumbled backward.

The young thugs didn't rush to treat their father; they scrambled to find his gun.

Neal ran to his car, slid in, and fumbled with the key.

A bloody hand slapped the passenger window.

Neal pressed hard on the button that locked the doors.

One of the men yanked the door handle.

Neal hit the gas. The car roared and sped away. He passed the other two vehicles just down the road as the memory of what he had done replayed in his mind. He had shot a man—maybe killed him. *I told them how to fix their cars! They could do what I said and be chasing after me right now.* No, it was too soon, but still he glanced over his shoulder and then at the crimson handprint on the passenger window. His heart pounded as he pressed harder on the gas pedal.

South of Eugene, an increasing number of cars dotted I-5, but he managed to weave around the abandoned vehicles.

Dozens of people walked along the road toward the city. Women, men, and even children waved for his help, but the memory of the shooting seared his thoughts. Neal couldn't bring himself to stop and help even the most innocent-looking individuals. He continued north, with a wary eye on the rearview mirror.

Just outside of Eugene the odor of burning rubber and plastic irritated his nose. He couldn't spot any fire, but the scent drifted on the air. When he rounded the next hill, several columns of gray and black smoke climbed above the trees. As he entered Eugene, a wall of flame weaved across much of the city.

* * *

Rural Chelan County, Washington, Sunday, September 4th

Still sitting, Conner slid away from the corpse. Death had never been so palpable. It had always been a closed coffin in a mortuary. He recalled his mother's death. One day she left home to buy groceries, and the next she lay in a coffin, never to return home again. He had cried tears of loss that day.

Conner had wanted to see her, and say some sort of goodbye, but his body had refused to lift from the pew.

Before today he had never stared into the face of death, but in less than two hours, he had looked into the sightless eyes of three bodies. Three people. *God, why did this happen?*

Had his mother looked so dead?

Again he turned away and gagged.

For several moments he considered what could be done. He pulled out his phone and tried to call but still had no service. With a shake of the head, he concluded that for this family, he could do nothing except return to civilization and report their passing.

He stood and stepped away but stopped. There was one more thing he could do for this unfortunate man. He avoided looking at the corpse as he grabbed it by the belt and a cool stiff hand. With a grunt, Conner pulled the body off the road. Then, using a tarp from his backpack, he covered the man.

Conner drank water and then repacked his gear but left his phone out. He flung his rifle over one shoulder and looked into the blue sky. "God … Are you there? Can you hear me? What's happened here?"

No answer thundered from the heavens, so he continued his trek toward civilization.

* * *

Rural Lewis County, Washington, Sunday, September 4th

Gruff wouldn't stop barking at the horses, so Drake pulled him back to the house and shut the doggie door with the metal plate. Then he returned to the living room and stared at the phone. *How do you look up a number without a computer?* As he glanced about the room, his gaze fell upon an end table beside his dad's favorite chair. He recalled his father kept a phonebook in a drawer.

Drake browsed the unfamiliar pages and discovered that the number wasn't listed under power or electric company. It took Drake several frustrating minutes to find what he needed. He lifted the receiver to his ear.

No dial tone.

It was an old-fashioned phone with no electric plug. Even without power, it should work. He tapped the plungers, picked it up, and shook it. He turned it upside down and sideways, but nothing seemed wrong. It just didn't work.

Why does Dad keep this ancient thing?

Briefly, he considered banging it against something.

After an angry sigh and a few more shakes of the phone, he thought of trying to start the generator or using one of the more modern landline phones. His dad had shown him once how to connect the generator. Drag it outside, flip the special switch in the breaker box, and use the special cable to hook it up to the house electric system.

Visions of lights blinking, sparks flying, and the house burning down flitted through his head. The power would be back on soon.

Drake let his gaze drift over the dark and messy living room. Would his dad think he caused the power outage? Perhaps he would if he came home now and saw the mess from the party. He could almost hear his dad say, "What did you do, blow every circuit breaker in the house?" Drake was pretty sure the power outage covered at least a few homes but didn't want to have to explain that to an angry dad. Before his father got home, Drake needed to finish his chores and clean the house.

Drake hurried from the house with Gruff right behind. He scanned the area for the horses and spotted them in the apple orchard. Gruff now seemed oblivious to the horses, so Drake grabbed a bucket and hurried to his chores with the dog following. Hand pumping the water made his chores take twice as long. He rubbed tender spots on his palms.

When he finished, Drake jogged toward the Hamilton house a few hundred yards down the road. Why hadn't they noticed that their horses were out? At least, after he told them, he could turn his attention to housecleaning. The day might still work out.

An eight-foot, wrought-iron fence blocked entry to the Hamilton farm from the road, but normally the gate stood wide open. As he turned into the driveway, Drake slowed to a walk. The gate stood closed and locked with a chain.

While this way was blocked, only a few strands of electric fence, trees, bramble, and bushes stood between his place and the Hamiltons'.

He ran back to his farm and grabbed gloves and clippers from the barn. Then he hiked over a small knoll near the house into a small wooded area. Drake cut through the bramble to the wire of the electric fence. Sweating and bleeding from several cuts, Drake tapped at the wire.

No zap.

He slid through, ran to the Hamilton home, and pressed the doorbell.

Nothing.

He knocked on the door. After a few moments, he banged again. Hearing no movement from inside, he walked around the house and peered in each window. He felt like a burglar checking out a target. With a frustrated grunt, he concluded no one was home. *What should I do about the horses?* He knew that chasing them would only scare the animals away, so he went to the neighbor's barn and poured grain into a bucket.

It took more patience than Drake thought he possessed, but eventually he lured the horses into the old corral behind his house. Then he filled a galvanized tub by hand-pumping gallons of water into buckets.

Sweat beaded on his forehead and ran into his eyes, stinging them closed. He wiped his face with his shirt, massaged his now blistered hands, and plopped down on the back steps. He should get the horses hay from the Hamiltons' barn, but that would entail several trips through the bramble. The neighbors would certainly be home soon.

No, right now he needed to clean the house.

Stepping through the back door, he glanced at the full laundry basket. With the power out, at least he didn't have to do that. Next, he came to the sink full of dirty dishes.

I'm really tired of pumping water.

Washing dishes with cold water seemed harder, especially the greasy ones. Normally, the dishwasher dried the dishes, but now he spent extra time wiping them with a towel. It seemed forever before he finished and dragged himself to the living room.

There, a dozen bowls and glasses from the party awaited him. He sighed. *Next party I'm using only disposable stuff.* He collected the items, found more in his room and a cup in Conner's, and returned to the kitchen for more dish washing and drying. Finally done with every bowl, glass, spoon, knife, and fork, he returned to the living room.

How do you clean a carpet without a vacuum? Drake closed his eyes. *Please God, I could really use a vacuum.* When he opened his eyes, Gruff was eating bits of food from the floor.

"Good boy."

Still, he retrieved a broom and swept the carpet where Gruff hadn't done his best work. Then Drake rubbed spots with a wet rag, and finally plucked fragments of popcorn and chips with his fingers.

As he stood from cleaning the carpet, he noticed dried spills and crumbled chips on the furniture. Determined to erase any hint of the party, Drake used a wet rag to wipe every surface. Then he bagged all the trash and hauled it out.

Perhaps all of this might prove to his father and older brother that he could be responsible.

Exhausted, Drake dragged himself to the living room and slumped into a chair. Now all he had to do was wait for his dad and brother to come home.

* * *

Lane County, Oregon, Sunday, September 4th

The city of Eugene burned. A line of flame rose along the south end of town. Winds fanned the inferno and blew black, acrid smoke across the freeway.

Neal's car remained the only vehicle moving. He shut the windows, to block the smoke and the growing cries of people.

On his left, a large American flag fluttered in the direction of the freeway. The winds were blowing the inferno his way. In some places, small fires already burned beside the road, but the wall of flame remained hundreds of yards away. Ahead, on his left, dozens of people jumped over the concrete barrier and ran across the lanes to escape the blaze.

Neal eased off the gas pedal to avoid hitting anyone. The memory of the gunfight remained fresh and raw in his mind, preventing him from stopping to assist others. Perhaps there wouldn't be another gun-toting thug, but groups of people were already forming along the highway. A mob driven by fear and flames might arise in an instant.

Weaving past cars and people, Neal crept along at twenty miles per hour, yet he needed to go faster to avoid the fire and not be surrounded by panicked people. Were his boys safe? He yearned to be home.

A man with a backpack ran across the highway, followed by a woman holding the hands of two children.

Farther down the road, another woman sprinted across in her bathrobe.

Three deer dashed past the woman.

As Neal rounded a curve, a wall of flame greeted him. Blown by the wind across the freeway, the fire engulfed the cars and trucks ahead.

He pressed the brake and slid to a stop.

A fist slammed against the driver's side window.

* * *

Rural Chelan County, Washington, Sunday, September 4th

Conner's feet hurt and the rifle sling dug into his shoulder.

How far had he walked? How much time had passed?

He had seen three dead people earlier in the day and not one living person. Those were the only facts that concerned him now. He shook his head and stared at the pavement, trying to shake the images of the dead from his mind.

On a holiday weekend people should be driving along the road, but for mile after mile, he saw no one. No planes flew overhead. No distant horns. No backfires or gunshots.

The screech of a hawk prompted Conner to lift his gaze. He spotted no bird in the sky, but when his gaze returned to the road, he noticed a pickup, with a boat and trailer behind, less than a half mile away.

"Hello!" Conner shouted and waved his arms as he ran toward the vehicle.

No sound came from the gray truck. It wasn't moving. The boat was just the right size for a couple of guys and a day of fishing. The driver must have been headed for the lake where Conner's truck remained, but why had they stopped?

Out of breath, he slowed to a jog and then walked as he drew near. The gray pickup sat silent and still on the road's shoulder.

"Is anyone here?" Conner looked about. Coming out this way, guys often drank too much coffee or beer and needed to stop for a short walk into the woods. "Hello. Anyone here? Uh … there's a wreck back up the road."

The breeze rustled in his ears.

Feeling like a car prowler, Conner tried both doors and found them locked. *Did the truck break down? Did they run out of gas?* He couldn't see the gauge.

Certain the driver would soon return, Conner considered waiting, but there were no side roads for miles. If he continued toward town, he should meet anyone returning to this truck. So, as the sun continued its trek across the sky, Conner continued his trek toward town.

Several hours later, as the shadows deepened, he thought of camping for the night, but for perhaps the first time in his life, he felt the need to talk to someone. Despite hunger and fatigue, he continued along the lonely road.

No moon rose to push back the growing blackness. Only a few stars dotted the night sky when Conner spotted something a couple of hundred yards down the road. At first, he thought it might be another vehicle but then wondered if it were a large animal, like a bear.

Conner eased the rifle off his shoulder.

Whatever it was, it didn't move.

Over the next few minutes, he stepped closer.

As his eyes adjusted to the night, he crept nearer until finally able to confirm that another auto sat silently along the road. This vehicle was smaller than the first, a two-door sedan.

"Hello? Is anyone there?"

Just like earlier, this vehicle appeared to have simply stopped and the driver had disappeared.

"Are you okay? Did you run out of gas?"

He edged forward but couldn't see anyone. Still, he decided to talk as if he did. "Uh … I need to get to town." He crept nearer and pointed up the road. "My truck broke down at the lake and there's a wreck."

Now next to the car, he knew no one remained inside. Conner tried the driver's door. It opened. The keys hung from the ignition.

Feeling like a car thief, he left his rifle by the door, sat down, and turned the key.

Lights came on. The gas gauge showed over half a tank, but the engine emitted no sound.

Just like his truck, the lights and gauges worked but not the engine. *That's weird.*

The dim light from the dash revealed a book and half-eaten candy bar on the passenger seat. Had they left suddenly? He picked up the book and it fell open, revealing it to be a Bible.

Memories of his mother reading Bible stories at bedtime flashed through his mind. He set the book down. He didn't need a Bible; he needed a ride home to the little brother he had left alone.

He stood next to the sedan, wishing someone would come along. He wanted to tell the authorities about the dead family. Certainly, they could explain the broken and abandoned vehicles. Couldn't they? "Help. Somebody? Anybody?"

"Hoo?" An owl called.

Tingles rippled along Conner's spine. Panic surged within him. What had happened to the world?

He ran toward town.

* * *

Lane County, Oregon, Sunday, September 4th

Neal turned in panic. A man with wild, crazed eyes stared through the driver's side window. Then he slammed his fist against the glass again.

Neal stomped the gas pedal, hurtling his vehicle toward the wall of flame. A yank of the steering wheel put the car into a skid into the other lane where it slammed into an abandoned sedan.

Crazy man, along with others, ran toward him.

Neal thrust the car into reverse; it flew backward, missing a woman by inches. Neal shifted into drive. Tires spun. The car sputtered and then roared down the freeway in the wrong direction.

Weaving around abandoned cars until he came to an onramp, he exited the freeway. In addition to shooting a man, he had now committed hit and run and sped down the freeway in the wrong direction. *Only criminals have days like this.*

Driving along side streets lined with suburban shops and homes, his breathing returned to near normal. As his mind cleared, a rattling sound from the right front of the car caused his gut to wrench.

Ahead stood a stop sign. He slowed and looked for people. This might be the place to pause and examine the damage.

He rolled forward.

An old pickup raced across the intersection in front of him.

Neal gasped and slammed on the brakes. Cautiously, he eased the vehicle forward and then rolled to a stop along the curb.

Breathe normally.

Neal looked over his shoulder. The pickup driver either knew how to fix an auto latch-up or the old truck had no electronics. *Driving defensively is still a good idea.* He grinned but wasn't sure why.

After taking a deep breath, he examined the area around him. Small shops with dark windows lined the street. Several recessed doorways provided hiding places. Smoke from the west drifted into this seemingly deserted area south of Eugene. Lifting an arm, Neal wiped his nose on a sleeve.

He needed to inspect the front of his car but didn't want to leave the vehicle or turn it off. Neal gritted his teeth as memories of the thug bleeding on the pavement returned. He looked around while keeping a tight grip on his pistol. He didn't want to shoot anyone over a damaged car, but he'd fight before allowing anyone to take it from him.

Seeing no one, Neal shifted into park and, without turning off the car, cracked open the door. After a glance all around, he jumped from the vehicle and raced to the front. Smoke hung heavy in the air. The right corner light hung loose, and the front fender had been torn and pushed close to the tire, but not against it. He smiled. The car remained drivable.

Then he heard the hissing sound.

Neal slid the pistol into the holster of his jacket and leaned close. The sweet smell of anti-freeze hit him before he spotted the tiny puncture in the radiator. The damage had almost certainly occurred when he hit the other car but such details didn't concern him. The fluid would leak out, causing his car to overheat and die. That concerned him.

He stood straight. Smoke from the burning city drifted along the street as he considered what to do.

On the far side of the road, a man stood in a doorway and watched. One hand hung empty by the man's side, but the other remained hidden in the entryway.

Neal edged around to the front of the car. With each step, he became a larger target.

"How come that car runs?" the man asked.

Without a word, Neal sidestepped toward the driver's door.

"Don't run off. Just tell me how come your car works."

"Try disconnecting the battery for a few seconds." Neal threw open the driver's door, jumped in, yanked the car into drive, and hurried down the road. A glance at the dash told him what he feared. The temperature light already glowed red.

Neal considered his options. He could stop and use something to plug the leak or find more fluid, but should he leave the car running? If he did, there was a strong possibility it would be stolen. If he turned the car off it might not restart. Even if it did restart, he might not be able to plug the leak, and more fluid was only a temporary fix. He decided to drive until the car died and then find another among the thousands of abandoned vehicles.

Five miles north, the engine shook, sputtered, and seized.

Neal put the vehicle in neutral and let the remaining momentum roll it to the curb.

He stuffed a few tools into the pack that served as his go-bag and grabbed his phone. With little hope of success, he turned it on.

No service.

Still, he tried to call home.

Nothing happened.

He drank some water and hefted the pack onto his back. The saying that long journeys begin with a single step entered his mind. His gaze drifted from the car to the endless road before him. He stepped forward, left the car behind, and hiked north.

As the sun continued its daily arc across the sky, Neal hiked along the side streets, always moving north and east in an effort to skirt the city and avoid the fires. More than a dozen times he passed abandoned cars, but each time he found no keys. *Considering the day I'm having, why not add car prowling and grand theft auto to my list of crimes?* He checked another car and shook his head. No keys. *I should have learned how to hotwire vehicles.*

Most of the day, others walked within sight of him, but Neal gave each a suspicious stare. Perhaps because of that, and the pistol in his hand, no one spoke to him as he trudged north.

Despite the gun, fear churned within him. Repeatedly, Neal looked right, left, and over his shoulders. Occasionally, he would turn completely around. It reminded him of the deer he often saw on the farm. They would nibble at the plants, raise their heads, and glance around. Then, nibble some more and look again. He wasn't a deer, but he felt hunted.

Breathing fast, he fingered the trigger of his pistol. He recognized the paranoia. Beth would tell him to trust God … have faith.

There were many things to fear in this dark new world, but right now nothing threatened him. Taking a slow, deep breath, he continued along the empty street.

Hours later, Neal walked along a country road somewhere northeast of Eugene. Spotting a grove of trees with bushes and bramble on two sides, he slid in and leaned back against one of the trunks. As the sun slid below the distant horizon, he hid within and stared into the growing darkness.

Day two

Lane County, Oregon, Monday, September 5th

Unable to rest, Neal sat on his sleeping bag, rocking back and forth with the pistol in his hand as stars drifted among auroras.

Beauty danced in the sky, but it also meant that the Earth's magnetosphere remained crippled and more damage had been inflicted upon the electrical systems and technology.

He felt numb and cold, perhaps because of the night air.

In the hours since the CME first slammed the planet, Neal had confronted fire, thugs, and fear.

He had shot a man.

Images of people fleeing the fires and grabbing at his car in panic flashed through his mind.

What were his sons facing? How were his sons doing? Guilt welled within him and twisted his gut. He should be home, but he had failed them, just as he had failed Beth when he hadn't protected her from the mugger. He should have been there, but he hadn't been, and she had bled out alone on a cold, gray sidewalk.

Now the world had fallen apart, and he cowered in the bushes hundreds of miles from his family.

Cowering? Am I a coward? No, but I am afraid. He recalled an old pastor saying that worry was a symptom of a lack of faith. There were things Beth feared, such as snakes and lightning, but she didn't worry about them or anything else. She had often whispered to him, "Let not your heart be troubled." Beth had faith. He had … nothing really.

After Beth was murdered, he withdrew from people, even his sons. Was that because of fear … fear of more pain? He wasn't certain but knew that fear grew within him. She would tell him to fight the fear. Thinking of Beth, sleep overtook him.

* * *

The sun warmed Neal's cheek, bringing him gradually to wakefulness. He rubbed his face and eyes, and stared into a clear blue sky. His attitude brightened with the rising sun. Again, he thought of his wife. He imagined how it would be if she were with him now. She would be afraid for her boys and anxious to get home, but she wouldn't worry about herself.

Neal ate an MRE, drank water, and prepared for a day of hiking. He pulled a map from his pack and stared at it as the gut-wrenching realization hit him. He had only a vague idea of his location.

His heart pounded.

No. Don't panic. There will be road signs. He breathed, deep and slow. *All I have to do is walk north until I reach the Columbia River.* He could almost hear Beth again saying, "Let not your heart be troubled."

The road before him veered roughly north amid farms and ranches. He didn't think he could reach Portland with one day of walking, but he could reach Salem and then Portland the next day. He might arrive home in three days, perhaps less if he really tried.

* * *

Rural Chelan County, Washington, Monday, September 5th

Conner walked until fatigue forced him to stop, then he dozed among the trees near the edge of the road and watched the northern lights once again fill the sky. When he felt rested, he continued his journey. As he drew nearer to town, his phone still showed no bars, but, as the new day dawned, he knew only a few miles remained between him and civilization.

Since he had hunted and fished in the area several times, he knew of a convenience store just a few miles ahead at the junction with the state highway. From there he would be able to report the accident and call a tow truck. Buoyed by that fact, he shifted the rifle to his other arm, adjusted the straps of his pack, and hurried onward.

The cool of morning lingered as he neared the junction and dashed across the road. Only when he reached the far side did it occur to him that no vehicles traveled along the highway, no cars were parked in front of the store, and none stood beside the gas pumps. Quickly he crossed the lot and grabbed the door handle. It clanked and barely moved.

Locked? Conner yanked on the other door with the same result. The sign said they opened at six in the morning during the summer. He didn't need a watch to tell him it was later than that. Leaning close, he peered into the dark store. Everything looked neat and normal. He banged on the window, but no one came.

Seeing a nearby spigot, he thought to top off his water bottles, but a turn of the valve brought only gurgles. Mumbling curses, he walked around the building, searching for some sort of answer but found none.

Moments later, he stood on the gravel edge of the highway and stared in the direction of the nearest town. He drank water from a bottle in his pack and sighed. He would need to hike a few more hours.

About a mile down the road, Conner came upon an empty pickup truck along the shoulder of the road. The hair on the back of his neck stood as he walked around it. Fear welled within him. This was the third abandoned vehicle he'd found. It couldn't be a coincidence.

With panic surging within him, Conner ran down the road.

Only when exhaustion forced him did he slow to a walk. He struggled to find some logical answer. Where were the people? Conner recalled a church camp years ago. A speaker had talked about the rapture, where all Christians would be taken to heaven before the great tribulation. He hadn't been to church much since his mother died, and he never read the Bible. He hadn't thought about God in years. Had the rapture happened and God passed him by? Was this the start of the tribulation?

As the sun neared its zenith, Conner reached the edge of a small town. He didn't see anyone, but the smell of barbecue hung over the street like an invitation. He followed his nose along a side road into a small subdivision.

Growls from his stomach led to visions of hamburgers, hot dogs, and steaks, which prompted more grumbles. In anticipation, he continued past several middle-class homes, seeing no one.

A woman strolled from the side of a nearby house holding a large cooler.

"Hello," Conner called. "Can you help me?"

She dropped the cooler and ran.

As he walked by the spot, Conner picked up the cooler and continued in the direction she had gone. He arrived at a small park with about thirty people of all ages, eating and playing ballgames. A covered pavilion stood at the center with four picnic tables. Several barbecues were in use on the side.

Perhaps the rapture hasn't happened. It all would have been so typical for a Labor Day weekend except for the four men, armed with rifles, watching as Conner approached.

An unarmed man, wearing an Oregon Ducks football jersey, stepped forward and held up his hand, motioning for Conner to stop.

The rifle remained on Conner's shoulder and he knew some would take it as a threat. He held out his arms with the cooler dangling from one hand. "I'm sorry I scared the woman. I was hunting in the mountains. My car wouldn't start; my phone won't work. I hiked out past several abandoned cars. Oh, and there's an accident. People died."

"Is anyone alive and injured there?" Ducks fan asked.

"No, all three are dead."

"Are you alone?" The Ducks fan glanced in the direction Conner came.

"Yes." Conner felt uneasy. "I'm not here to harm anyone."

"No, I don't think you are." Ducks guy stepped forward and held out his hand. "My name is Jim. Leave your rifle with one of the guards, sit down, eat some food, and I'll catch you up on the collapse of civilization."

* * *

Rural Lewis County, Washington, Monday, September 5th

Drake awoke to a close-up view of Gruff's nose. The dog licked his face.

"Stop it!" Drake sat up, wiped his face, and stretched. He looked about the living room and realized that he had fallen asleep on the couch. Stiff and groggy, he stood and unlatched the doggy door.

Gruff hurried outside.

Drake checked the house. The power remained out and neither his dad nor brother had returned. *What's going on?* He had wanted time alone, but this had gone on too long. His dad or brother should be here.

He ate a quick bowl of cereal breakfast, using goat's milk. Then he fed their animals and the Hamiltons' horses.

Hot and sweating, he returned to the back porch.

Gruff nuzzled beside him.

"What should I do?" Drake patted the dog. "Where are Dad and Conner? Why is the power off?" For several moments he sat on the back steps and thought. "Come on, we're going for a walk."

The Evans' farm sat near the top of a steep incline that overlooked the town of Riverbank. The hill had a name, Fremont, but he always called it "the hill." With Gruff on a leash, he ambled along a straight stretch of road in the direction of town.

The smell of smoke hung in the air as he walked. Since summer lingered, it wouldn't be a woodstove, and since he heard no fire trucks, it must be someone's burn pile. He gave it no further attention and continued his hike.

In the past, Riverbank had always seemed so close, but he had been walking for nearly ten minutes and only now reached the turn for Ashley's house. He paused and considered his options. Six homes were in view, and all seemed strangely quiet. No one else walked along the road, no cars moved, no noise at all.

"What are you doing?" A loud voice called.

* * *

Lane County, Oregon, Monday, September 5th

Earlier, Neal had seen others walking in the direction of Eugene and Portland, but for the last several hours, he walked alone along the country road. He shifted his backpack, moved the rifle to the other shoulder, and trudged on.

A few people worked the fields and vineyards with hand tools and wheelbarrows, but they seemed cautious, watching as he passed. Several were armed with rifles and pistols. He had no desire for a confrontation, and little desire for talk, so he pushed northward toward the Columbia River and his home beyond.

As the sun rose, heating the day, Neal looked for a shady area to stop and eat. He rounded a bend and spotted a hill topped with fir trees about a half mile ahead. On the road below sat a blue SUV.

Somewhere in the distance, a dog barked.

Neal approached the vehicle, slowing his pace as he neared. "Hello? Anyone there?" He looked at the car and trees as he fought fears of marauding criminal gangs and the traps they might set to steal his supplies.

Walking gave him too much time to think—and imagine the worst. He shook his head as if to clear it. As he walked around the car, he spotted the keys still inside. Excitement surged within him. He might be home in a few hours. Again he looked around, hoping to see no claimant of the vehicle or any thug willing to fight for it. With no one near, he pulled the tools from his pack and disconnected the battery.

With the cables back in place, Neal hurried to the driver's seat and turned the key. The starter clicked, dash lights flickered on and the seatbelt warning dinged annoyingly, but despite several tries, the engine didn't turn over.

Discouraged, he exited the vehicle, kicked the tire, and climbed to the top of the hill. After calming down, he ate lunch in the shade of the fir trees.

Out of sight, the dog maintained its relentless barking.

As he ate his energy-bar-and-water lunch, he wondered if he'd been unlucky with the car or whether the aurora of last night meant the Earth continued to be slammed by CMEs. He sighed, repacked his gear, and continued north.

The road dipped into a ravine where a creek cut along the bottom. Neal filtered the water into his bottles and then hiked up the far bank.

At the top of the slope, he spotted a white farmhouse about a half mile farther up the road on a nearby knoll. The two-story home included a porch that wrapped around at least two sides. A red barn stood behind it. As his gaze swept the area, he noticed a dog barking at the house.

Occasionally the animal moved and sunlight flashed off the chain that held it.

The dog wants something—food, water, off the chain … who knows? Why doesn't the owner check on the poor animal?

Neal would need to pass the house on his way north. Anxious to put the noisy beast behind him, he increased his pace. Minutes later, Neal stood at the driveway entrance to the farm. Going up to the house was a bad idea. It could be a trap. No, that was paranoid thinking. But, it remained a bad idea. The breeze thumped the gate against a fence post, almost inviting him to walk up to the home.

The dog whined.

Why did no one tend to the animal?

The owner might be deaf or gone.

Neal crept up the driveway. "Hello? Anyone home?"

What if the farmer returned? He might think I'm robbing the place. He might shoot me or sic the dog on me. Neal hesitated but couldn't leave the animal to die locked on a chain.

With his heart pounding in his chest, he stepped along the driveway but kept his pace slow and his hands visible. With each footfall on the gravel, he expected to hear a gunshot or have a dog lunge at him from nowhere. But everything remained peaceful, except for the clamor of the dog.

Neal continued up the rutted driveway. Near the top of the knoll, he veered off the lane, crossed a few feet of lawn, and walked up creaking steps to the front door. He knocked and waited, but no one answered. He knocked again, listened for movement but heard no one, and continued his walk along the squeaky porch. "Hello? I heard the barking and just thought I should check. Anyone home?" Trying not to look suspicious, he gazed in a window at an empty room.

When he turned the corner to the back, he locked eyes on the tan and black German Shepard about twenty feet away.

The dog stared at him in silence.

"Hey boy … girl, whatever, how're you doing?" Two empty bowls lay upside down near a simple doghouse.

The dog sat and shifted its gaze between Neal and the back door as if urging him to enter the home.

Neal edged along the porch. "Where's your master? Inside?"

The back door hung by a single hinge. The latch had nearly been torn from the door. Splintered wood littered the floor just inside. With a soft push, he eased the door open. "Hello? Anyone home? I'm coming in."

The dog whimpered.

The refrigerator stood open, along with every cabinet. Condiment containers, herbs, and spices littered the floor. Nearby, the pantry shelves stood bare.

"I didn't break your door." *Or mess up your kitchen.* "I'm here to help if you need it."

Neal continued past the laundry and bathroom and into the living room. There, in a recliner, sat an elderly man. He stared at the black television screen with unseeing eyes. Tubes laced to the old man's nose from a nearby oxygen tank.

Floorboards creaked.

"He's dead."

* * *

Rural Chelan County, Washington, Monday, September 5th

Conner sank his teeth into a juicy hamburger and enjoyed the savory beef, tomato, and mayo. Then he locked his gaze on Jim, the man sitting across from him. "So, the storm on the sun knocked out the power in the Pacific Northwest?"

"Everywhere, we think."

Conner felt as if he had been punched. "Everywhere?"

Jim nodded.

"If the power is out all over the planet, won't there be food shortages and starvation?"

Again Jim nodded. "I'd guess that millions will starve."

"But you're having a picnic and feeding me?"

"You were hungry, so we gave you food." Jim shrugged. "Besides, the hamburger meat, mayonnaise, and bread won't last long without refrigeration."

Conner tried to grasp the magnitude of the disaster, but it overwhelmed him. "The situation is going to get bad very quickly." He bit off another mouthful of burger. "Thanks for the food," he mumbled around the bread and beef.

As Conner swallowed, guilt soured the taste. *I left Drake alone.* He prayed that his dad had returned home before the storms hit.

Conner had traveled about 250 miles from home to hunt. He knew a person could travel about four miles per hour across level ground. If he walked about twelve hours each day, it would take him five days to reach home.

He grinned inwardly. That was the first time in his life a math story problem had been useful.

His amusement faded. He recalled the mountains between him and home. His trip wouldn't be along level ground.

*   *   *

Rural Lewis County, Washington, Monday, September 5th

Drake turned.

"Aren't you the Evans' boy?" An ancient man, maybe sixty years old, with thin gray hair ambled toward him.

Drake stepped back.

Gruff growled.

"I haven't seen you in years." The old man smiled. "You're Beth's boy, right?"

Drake relaxed a bit. "Yeah, she was my mother."

The old man nodded. "She was a good person. I'm Pastor Wayne. You went to my church before your mom passed away."

Drake glanced at the nearby community church.

From the porch of the home beside the church, a younger man shouted. "Dad, please get out of the sun. You don't know what it might be doing to you."

Pastor Wayne looked back. "That's my boy, Dan. He thinks the sun is going to kill us all."

"That's silly."

"I agree, but trying to convince Dan is hard." Wayne smiled. "So, why are you casually walking around while the world's falling apart?"

Drake had no clue what Pastor Wayne meant. "The power is out. I wondered why."

The old man nodded his head a few times and rubbed his chin. "Where's your dad?"

Drake felt nervous telling the truth. He was alone but didn't want to admit it. He'd been taught to say that his dad was in the bathroom or the barn. "He's at home, Conner, everyone they're at home."

"I'm not sure." Pastor Wayne tilted his head. "Is he?"

Dan stepped from the house. "Dad, come back inside."

Wayne waved him off. "Son, just because there was a storm on the sun doesn't mean we're all going to die."

"Storm on the sun?" Drake repeated and took a step back.

"Yeah, probably knocked out power, computers, and cars everywhere."

"That's impossible." Drake took more steps back.

"Smell that acrid smoke?" Pastor Wayne asked. "Do you hear any fire trucks racing to put it out?"

The son jogged across the road to his father. "Come on, Dad. Let's get inside."

"Yeah, I've got to go." Drake pulled on Gruff's leash and ran along the road toward town.

A hundred yards down the road, Drake caught his first view of Riverbank. Smoke swirled into the air from two house fires about a half mile away, but, as the old man said, he heard no alarms. From his vantage point on the hill, he should have been able to see firefighters, but all he saw were people standing and watching.

He continued along the road until he could see the freeway. A dozen cars and trucks were strung out along the portion of the highway visible to him, but, as if time had frozen, none moved. Only then did Drake see a group of people walking among the stationary vehicles.

Was it possible? Shielding his eyes with a hand, Drake lifted his gaze to the sky. *Had power, phones, and cars stopped working worldwide? No TV?*

Drake could pump water by hand, but what about most people? *What about food? Did he have enough for the winter?*

Fear coursed through Drake and he ran toward home.

*   *   *

Lane County, Oregon, Monday, September 5th

Neal spun around at the sound of a male voice. He stumbled backward and pulled his pistol. A young man and woman, a little older than Conner's eighteen years, stood in the far entry to the living room. The man had a duffle bag over one shoulder and a crowbar in his hand. The woman held a bat.

"We didn't kill him," the woman added hastily.

The old man looked dead, but, just in case, Neal bent over and, keeping one hand on his pistol, poked the body with his free hand.

The young man pointed with the crowbar. "That's how we found him."

Neal's gaze shifted back and forth between the weapons in their hands.

"He was dead when we broke in." Her words were pleading. "He was right there in the chair like you see him now."

"We're just looking for food." The man tapped the bag with his crowbar. "We can give you some if you need it."

Neal shook his head. "How did he die?"

The man shrugged. "He was old."

"I know he had a pacemaker," the woman added. "With every other electrical thing going on the blink, well, all I know for sure is, we didn't do it."

"You knew him?"

"I'm a visiting nurse." She frowned. "I took care of him."

Neal shook his head. *And when you thought he was probably dead, you preyed upon him like a vulture.*

"Can we go?" the woman asked.

With a wave of the pistol, Neal signaled for them to leave.

They ran out the front door.

For several moments, Neal stood looking at the open door and the body of the old man. What had become of the world? Gradually, he retraced his steps through the ransacked kitchen and out the back door.

The dog stared at him.

"Well, what's to become of you?"

The animal stood and wagged its tail.

Neal retreated to the kitchen, found two bowls and using one, dipped water from the toilet tank into it. He poured dog food into the other. Then he approached the dog with slow cautious steps and slid the bowls the last few inches. "Here you go. I'll bet you could use this."

The animal eagerly drank the water and then consumed the food. Moments later it had licked the last from both bowls and sat.

The two stared at each other for a moment.

"I really don't need a dog. I already have one at home." The best thing Neal felt he could do was provide the mutt a chance of survival by releasing it. Neal inched forward. "Good dog." He ran his hand along the chain. "Are you feeling better?" Sunlight caught a blue tag and it flashed. The dog moved and Neal spotted the name, "Ginger." He unsnapped the chain.

The dog sprinted into the house, followed by Neal.

In the living room, Ginger sniffed around the body of her master.

"I had nothing to do with his death, Ginger. Sorry."

Ginger lay near her master while Neal searched the rest of the house for useful items.

In the closet of the master bedroom, Neal found a shotgun and eight loose shells. Staring at the gun, he considered whether he now preyed upon the dead man, as the young couple had done.

No, he had come here to help, not steal food. The gun could do the old man no good and might save Neal during the long and dangerous journey ahead. Perhaps it was a rationalization, but in a world falling apart and going crazy, it was one he could live with.

He slung the shotgun over one shoulder and pocketed the shells. Then he grabbed the quilt from the bed. In the living room, the dog remained beside her master. He had taken longer at the farmhouse than he intended, but before leaving, Neal spread the quilt over the old man. Then he bent down and patted the dog. "Goodbye, Ginger. I hope things go well for you. I've got to keep going north to my boys and home." Neal returned to the kitchen, dropped the bag of dog food on the floor where Ginger could get to it, and then headed out along the road.

A hundred yards from the farm, Ginger galloped up to him and walked alongside.

"Like I said earlier, Ginger, I don't need a dog." Neal pointed back toward the house. "Go home!"

The dog's tongue rolled out and she panted.

"Go home!"

She barked and sat.

"Please, go home."

She cocked her head and seemed to grin.

Neal sighed. "Okay, you win." He returned to the house, crammed the half-empty dog food bag into his pack, and headed back out along the country road with Ginger leading the way.

* * *

Rural Chelan County, Washington, Monday, September 5th

Conner imagined his route home. He would follow the Columbia River south to Interstate 90 and head west across the Cascade Mountains, and down into Seattle. Then he would turn south toward home. *Easy to say and easy to drive but a long walk.* Conner took another bite of burger and turned to Jim. "If you don't mind, I'll eat and run. Well, walk actually."

As he chewed on the burger it occurred to Conner that the trip would be quicker if he used a bicycle. "Jim, do you know anyone who would sell or trade with me for a bike?"

"I'll ask around." Jim walked toward the first cluster of people, stopped and talked for a moment, and then moved on to the next.

When Conner finished eating, he scanned the area and, within seconds, spotted Jim talking with another man.

With a wave of the arm, Jim signaled for him to come over. "This is Chris. He has a bike."

The guy was perhaps a few years older than Conner but with a wedding ring on his finger. Conner held out his hand, and they shook.

"I race bikes and have a really good one. It cost me over five thousand dollars." Chris drew a deep breath. "But I'll trade it for that rifle you walked in with."

Conner shook his head. "I'd buy it from you, but I only have about three hundred dollars."

Chris shook his head. "What's money worth now?"

Conner shrugged as he pondered the question.

Jim walked away with Chris but returned a moment later. "I have another idea. There's a strange old guy in town named Randolph. Some say he's a millionaire. He collects stuff and sells all kinds of things in his thrift store; it's the largest in town. I've seen bikes in there before."

"Yeah, but do you think he'd be in the store on a day like this?"

"I've seen him there on Christmas and Thanksgiving. If people want to buy, he'll be there."

After Conner retrieved his rifle from the guards, he followed the directions Jim had written on a scrap of paper into town.

It didn't take long to find the brick building with a large painted sign, "Randolph Thrift and Gift."

A bell hanging over the door swayed and dinged as Conner entered. The dark store smelled of dust, old books, and musty clothes. An elderly man with thinning white hair, and wearing a sweater, ambled toward the front.

"Hi, are you Randolph? I'm looking for a bicycle."

He nodded. "I've got about a dozen bikes—kids ones, dirt bikes, racing… What exactly are you looking for?"

"I don't need a racing bike." Conner described the trip that lay before him. "I can spend maybe three hundred dollars."

"That little?"

"That's about all I've got." Conner regretted revealing how much money he had. He did have a credit card through his dad but didn't want to have to explain spending hundreds of dollars for a used bike. But, if it got him home, it would be worth it. "With the power still out can you take a credit card?"

"Nope. Can't process it. Cash only until the government gets things back to normal."

How long will that take? "Okay, show me what you have."

Randolph ambled toward the back, leaving Conner to wonder if he should follow. After a few minutes, he returned with a very used, pink and rust adult-sized street bike.

"That's a three-hundred-dollar dollar bike?"

"It is today." Randolph shrugged. "Tomorrow it might cost six hundred dollars."

Conner pulled out his wallet and counted the bills. "I've got $287."

Randolph grinned. "I guess I'm feeling generous today." He held out his hand.

As Conner handed over the money, he asked, "Can I get a pump for the tires?"

"Sure." Randolph smiled. "In exchange for that watch on your wrist."

Conner gave up the watch that had been a birthday gift from his father. Randolph might be a millionaire, but money might already be worthless. Just outside the store, Conner mounted the bike and pedaled south, out of town, with the rifle over one shoulder and the pack on his back. The uneven weight caused him to sway and weave a bit, but the pavement was wide, flat, and empty. Still, out of a lifetime of habit, he stayed on the shoulder to the right.

With the blue sky above and the Columbia River flowing just west of the highway, providing a reliable source of water, he felt good about this part of the trip. Crossing the mountains that loomed to the west was a worry he would try to put off for as long as possible.

It didn't work. Biking gave Conner too much time to think. His father was in Nevada. He had left Drake alone at home, and it would take him days to get back there.

He hunched his shoulders, shifting the weight on his back, and pedaled faster.

Worry pushed him forward, but fatigue slowed him. Conner prided himself on being physically fit, but it had been years since he last rode a bike any distance. *Slow and steady wins the race.* As he continued south the words became a mantra, repeated in his head.

The sun had fallen below the western mountains when Conner passed a sign welcoming him to the city of Wenatchee. He continued south, trying to decide whether he should skirt around or go through the town when he noticed a large homemade sign directing refugees who needed assistance to turn off the highway.

He hadn't passed many people during the day. How many refugees could there be?

The next sign read, "Local Church Refugee Assistance." An arrow pointed left.

Conner pedaled on until he spotted a gathering of a couple of hundred people in a wooded park by the river. He dismounted and joined a dozen others walking toward the entrance.

In some ways, it reminded him of where he ate lunch. Children played, while adults gathered in groups or cooked food on barbecue grills. But there were many more people here, and not everyone looked friendly. He shook his head. Like him, they were all probably just trying to get home. He had a rifle over his shoulder and hadn't shaved or bathed in three days. He probably looked like trouble to those around him.

Conner's fear of gangs subsided when he noticed two police officers strolling among the refugees and another cop near the entrance.

As he approached, the officer held up his hand. "No guns in the park."

Conner stopped and nodded. "Fair enough. I won't go in." He threw a leg over his bike as others walked past him.

A shot boomed behind him.

People shoved and ran.

Conner fell to the ground.

*   *   *

Rural Lewis County, Washington, Monday, September 5th

As he sprinted back toward home, Drake changed his mind and turned the corner to Ashley's house. Out of breath, he slowed to a walk, and then stopped and bent over, panting. *More exercise, fewer video games.*

Gruff pranced anxiously around him.

When his breathing returned to near normal, he continued his trek. Ashley lived on the north side of Fremont Hill toward the bottom and much closer to the freeway. She had to have seen stalled cars and plumes of smoke. It probably unnerved her, just like it did him, but her parents should be there.

Yeah, her parents were probably home, and he should get back to the farm. No. He rejected the idea. She would be happy he stopped by to check on her. The thought made him smile and again he ran.

Gruff's tongue hung out as he jogged beside Drake.

Within a couple of minutes, he spotted Ashley's yellow house. Three motionless cars were visible on the freeway. Beyond it, a grass fire had blackened the slope down to the river and still smoldered.

Drake pressed the doorbell and then slapped his forehead. *Idiot, the power is out.* He knocked and heard movement inside. The door opened a crack with the chain still latched. Ashley stood just inside with red, puffy, eyes. Her blonde hair seemed limp against her head.

"Hi!" Drake smiled. "I just thought I'd check on you."

"Thanks." Ashley unlatched the chain and opened the door but didn't invite him in.

"Are you okay?" Worried, Drake stepped closer. "Are your parents here?"

"No, not yet." She wiped her face with a hand. "What about your father and brother?"

Drake shook his head. "Why don't you come to my place? We'd be safer together."

"No, I need to wait here for my parents."

"They know where I live. Leave them a note."

She shook her head. "They'll be here soon."

"They may never come," he blurted.

Ashley slapped him.

* * *

Linn County, Oregon, Monday, September 5th

Using road signs, Neal continued his northward hike to Portland accompanied by Ginger. After several attempts to start abandoned cars, he gave up and concentrated on hiking. Using his self-winding watch and milepost signs, he estimated his speed at three miles per hour. That seemed an agonizingly slow pace even without thinking of his boys at home alone.

Together, Neal and Ginger hiked to the small town of Sweet Home, which seemed unharmed by recent events, but no cars moved along the streets, and many people walked in the roads. This didn't please Ginger. She growled at anyone who strolled nearby.

"Calm down, girl." But after a few more growls, Neal pulled paracord from his backpack and used it as a leash.

For several hours they hiked northwest, following the rural highway. As the sun slid below the trees, they reached the outskirts of Lebanon. Smoke hung in the air, and Neal had little desire to be in a larger town after dark, especially with a stolen shotgun over one shoulder. Perhaps such worries were a bit crazy, but it was a level of paranoia that Neal felt comfortable with.

Ginger led him to a lake where she drank while he filtered water into his bottles. Then they continued on and he soon discovered the source of the smoke. Several cars smoldered in a Walmart parking lot. A crowd swarmed near the doors like angry wasps.

Cautious, Neal approached, using distance and the vehicles in the parking lot to remain hidden as much as possible.

Ginger growled.

Neal knew he should stay away, but the looters were like some horrid accident repulsing yet drawing him in at the same time. When he stood as close as he dared, still many yards from the crowd, he stopped and watched.

Shattered glass doors left shards on the pavement. Looters were inside the store and more rushed in. Those who ran out carried mostly clothes and food. Neal grinned at the sight of a young man, about Conner's age, leaving with a game system. The system might already be burned out from the CME, but even if not, it would be a long time before he could use it.

As the young man jogged across the parking lot, the looters at the Walmart door started punching, shoving, scratching, and screaming. The chaos swirled away from the entrance. Several women skittered past Neal in their haste to flee.

Neal tugged on the paracord leash. "Come on, Ginger, let's get out of here." He jogged away from the Walmart in the general direction the women had gone, across a wide highway of abandoned cars to a grassy area beyond.

Tents and sleeping bags were scattered in the open space. Small groups of people clustered around cooking fires. Neal thought about joining them but decided to move a hundred yards away to a line of trees and bushes. In the last few days, humans had caused him more trouble than he cared to think about. Seclusion seemed his best option. Near a cluster of large fir trees, Neal tied Ginger's leash to a small pine and spread his tarp and sleeping bag.

As he dug through his backpack for the dog food, eight men swaggered into the meadow.

Everyone seemed to turn and stare at the new arrivals in dark leather jackets. Campers near the approaching group stepped back out of the way.

"Who has food for my friends and me?" The lead man, arms covered with tattoos, bellowed.

Ginger's hackles rose and she growled.

Neal pulled her close and whispered, "Quiet, girl." He tapped a hand against the pistol in his jacket and edged backward into the shadows.

From his dark vantage point slightly above the meadow, Neal watched the eight thugs march toward one of the campfires. One had a shotgun, another had a pistol. They pushed, shoved and badmouthed anyone in their way.

Ginger gave a low, menacing growl.

"We don't want a fight," Neal whispered. "If all they do is take some food and leave, that'll be okay."

When the thugs had stolen enough food, they gathered around a now deserted campfire to eat. Most of the refugees left; the few who remained stayed well away.

During the next hour, nightfall overtook everything. The campfires burned low and silence settled in the meadow. Neal remained hidden in the trees, confident he had remained unseen and thankful for the quiet. Ginger fell asleep, and eventually, Neal did also.

Sometime during the night, gunfire erupted.

*　　*　　*

Chelan County, Washington, Monday, September 5th

Conner hit the ground with a thud and someone fell on top of him. He wanted to stay low but not with his face in the dirt. "Get off."

"Sorry," a woman said. "I got pushed."

Three police officers ran past with guns ready.

In the dimming light, Conner grabbed what he thought was his bicycle and stood.

"That's mine." She pointed. "That old thing must be your bike."

More shots and screams rent the night.

Conner retrieved his bike. "Let's get out of here."

They pedaled fast and hard from the panic and shooting along a path away from the park. The light faded as the sun rested behind the Cascade Mountains, but while it lasted, Conner used it to assess his new biking partner. She looked to be about his age, with dark hair to the middle of her back. A bag hung from one shoulder, or it might have been a large purse. Other than that she had no provisions.

When he had finished taking her in, he dropped his gaze to the girl's bike. It looked lightweight, expensive, and, unlike Conner's, just the right size for her. He knew nothing about bike racing, but because of the nice bike, and her strong pedaling, Conner guessed cycling had been a hobby.

When they finally stopped, Conner figured they were somewhere just west of Wenatchee. "I'm Conner Evans. Do you have a place to stay tonight?"

"Madison Croft." She shook her head. "I hadn't planned … no, why?"

"See that convenience store? We can stay in the brush and tall grass beside it for the night and not be seen."

She stopped. "You go there. I'll stay near the gas station."

"Oh." Conner's face warmed with understanding. "I won't hurt you. We're both safer together."

Her gaze shifted to the rifle on his shoulder. "I'll stay here."

"Okay." He nodded and headed into the field. When he found a low spot where he could hide, Conner looked back at the station. Madison was gone.

"Please God, keep her safe." He laid the bike to one side and then knelt, spread his tarp, and unrolled his sleeping bag onto it. With the bike on his left and rifle on the right, he ate an energy bar supper and prepared to sleep.

Tired but tense, sleep came grudgingly to Conner. Wakefulness would slip away only to return like a punch in the gut at some sound in the night. Several times he listened, edgy with worry, but heard only distant voices or the hoot of an owl. Gradually he would slip back to sleep, only to wake again with his heart pounding in fear.

Sometime during the night, Conner awoke to the sound of breaking glass. He slipped from his sleeping bag and peeked above the grass. Several men with flashlights broke out the large window of the convenience store and, with much laughter, entered the building.

A dark figured hurried from the far side of the building into the grass.

Madison?

Moving fast and staying low, the dark figure neared Conner's campsite.

"Madison?" he called as loud as he dared.

The person turned and hurried toward him. Only when she crouched by his side could he see her well enough to know it was Madison.

"I'm glad you're still here," she whispered.

"I'm glad you're safe."

Together they watched as the men looted the store and disappeared into the darkness.

Conner slid low to the ground. "You can stay here if you want."

Madison sat curled into a tight ball. "Yeah. I guess that's a good idea."

"Do you have a sleeping bag?" Conner knew she didn't and she confirmed it with a shake of the head. "You can use mine. I've got a blanket I can use, but we'll need to share the tarp."

"Oh? Okay."

He sensed her hesitancy and fingered the tarp. "It keeps away the moisture from the ground." Conner looked back toward the station. "Did you leave your bike?"

"Yeah, we can get it in the morning."

After she settled inside the sleeping bag, he lay next to her and pulled up the blanket. Through the materials, his left arm touched her right. "If we're going to spend the night this close, I had a thought."

He felt her tense.

"We should get to know each other a bit. You know, talk."

"Okay." She let out a deep breath. "Where were you when the CME struck?"

"I guess it hit when I saw the northern lights." Conner explained about his hunting trip. "I only expected to be gone a couple of days. Now I feel awful about leaving my little brother, Drake, alone."

"Yeah. I'm worried about my parents."

"So, where were you when it hit?" Conner asked.

"I was headed to Pullman for my freshman year at WSU."

"Washington State, that's a good university."

"Yes." Madison turned toward him. "They have a good vet school. That's what I wanted to study." She sighed. "I'd been listening to an audiobook as I drove and only heard about the CME when I stopped for dinner Saturday evening."

"Did you turn around?"

"Yeah." Madison sighed. "I knew I didn't have enough time to reach home—"

"Where's home?"

"Olympia, but I wanted to get as close as I could."

Conner nodded, but it was too dark for her to see it. "I would have done the same thing. I'm from Riverbank so we're heading in the same direction. You're welcome to keep riding with me."

"I think that would be nice."

The conversation under the stars continued until Conner drifted off to sleep.

The sun woke him the next morning. He sat up and rubbed his face, eyes, and sore legs. The sleeping bag lay open and empty. Conner looked about for Madison. Her bike still leaned against a nearby rock with a lock through the spokes. She must be nearby.

Conner pulled two energy bars from his pack, rolled up the sleeping bag, shook the tarp, and tossed it over her bike.

He heard a noise behind him and turned.

A man with a pistol stepped into the clearing. "I thought I heard somebody. That rusty bike is worth more than your life, and the rifle is worth even more."

* * *

Rural Lewis County, Washington, Monday, September 5th

Drake stumbled back. Ashley's slap hurt both his feelings and his cheek.

"Don't say that!" Tears filled her eyes.

"Sorry," he mumbled.

She slammed the door.

Convinced he had said exactly the wrong thing, and that Ashley would never speak to him again, Drake slunk toward home with Gruff in the lead. As he walked, a sinking feeling grew within him. It was possible that his father and brother would never return. Panic filled him, and he ran.

Inside the house, he dropped to the floor, near tears with worry for his father, brother, and the words he'd said to Ashley.

Later, he fed Gruff and the other animals, pumped a few gallons of water for washing and drinking, and ate an apple and chips for supper. Exhausted, more from worry than work, he slipped into bed when darkness fell.

Still in the gloom of night, Drake awoke, sweating so much that the sheets were damp to the touch. He sat up as he recalled a memory that threatened to slip away. A long time ago, his father had gathered information into two binders, one orange and the other red. He tried to remember why that moment had been important. After several seconds, he shook his head and slumped back. As he drifted off to sleep, he recalled his father's words to him. "Read these." In the dream or fading memory, his father slid the binders onto the bookshelf in the office.

Drake grabbed the flashlight from the nightstand and ran to the office. The light fell on the binders still where he remembered them from years ago. He grabbed the orange one and opened it. The first page read, "Condition Orange. Read this when a specific threat, emergency, or alert has been identified."

The binders contained an instruction manual for the generator, rifle disassembly and cleaning pamphlets, and pages with bulleted action points written by his father. The first item seemed to jump out at him.

Close and lock the gate across the driveway.

How could he have been so foolish as to leave that open? Closing it might not stop someone from walking onto the property, but it would at least prevent them from driving to the front door.

He dressed in haste, found the key hanging with others near the front door, ran along the driveway, and locked the gate.

Then he returned to the office and continued reading by flashlight.

If power is out for a prolonged period, the generator is available. It can handle the normal household load, but more gas is used as the load increases. Use the generator to power the pump and fill water containers, charge radios and batteries, and keep the freezer cold. Accomplishing these tasks should take only a couple of hours of power per day.

"Keeping the freezer cold!" How much food had spoiled because he'd been too lazy and stupid to start the generator? He vowed to start it at dawn. A lump of sadness grew within as he continued to read.

During a prolonged electrical outage, don't use the generator at night or display electric lights after dark. Doing so shows you have a generator, gas, and probably other supplies. It makes you a target.

"Me, a target?" He gripped the rifle and read on.

If there is a chance of civil unrest, someone should be awake and on guard at all times.

"Well, that's not possible with just me here."

As the crisis continues, looting and violence will grow. Unlock the supply closet and select a gun you're familiar with. Keep it near you at all times. If you're on guard duty, keep it loaded and in your hands.

"People robbing and looting?" Drake slumped in the chair as he thought of all the food and supplies on the farm. How could he protect it? He looked across the office to the closet, or at least that's what it appeared to be. Eight years ago, his dad had remodeled the house, adding, among other things, the office where Drake sat. The door he now stared at was usually referred to as the supply closet. It occupied the space of a large walk-in closet or a very small bedroom. Except to prepare for an occasional fishing and camping trips or target shooting, Drake never entered.

The door was always locked, but a couple of years back, his father had shown him the location of the key—inside the cutout pages of a paperback book behind the office desk. Moments later, in the supply closet, Drake stared at ten rifles and nearly as many pistols.

He selected a Winchester thirty-thirty lever action rifle that his father had given him. He had shot cans, targets, and a few watermelons with the rifle. It felt natural in his hands.

He grabbed a box of ammo from the nearby shelf and then cast the beam of the flashlight around the room. There were more weapons—a bow with arrows, knives, several hatchets—and nearby shelves held packages of dehydrated food, camping gear, radios, and much more. Since the room had no window, he planned to return in the morning after starting the generator. Then he would have a good look at the available supplies.

Drake entered the living room and sat on the couch. He remembered more than once rolling his eyes at his father's preparations. *Thanks, Dad, for all you did, but please come home.*

With the rifle across his lap, he continued to read the orange binder until his eyes drooped and the paragraphs blurred into incomprehensible lines. The folder dropped to his lap.

He rested his eyes and pondered a thousand questions. Would his dad and brother ever return? How could he guard the farm alone? How much food did he have?

The tick of a nearby clock faded into dreams of family and friends together during better times.

In the dream, Gruff growled.

Drake struggled to open heavy eyes.

Gruff edged toward the front window. The hair on the back of his neck rose and he growled low.

Clutching the rifle, Drake jumped to his feet.

Day three

Lebanon, Oregon, Tuesday, September 6th

Clutching his pistol, Neal struggled to see in the predawn twilight. Ginger strained against her paracord leash, pulling the thin strand along his hand. Neal gripped with both hands to stop the dog, which continued to bark in the direction of the rapid gunfire. Neal scurried to a nearby tree, pulling the dog along behind him.

After a few minutes of rapid-fire shooting, silence returned to the darkness.

Neal waited in the trees for greater visibility that arrived with the morning, gray and silent, like death itself.

A dozen bloodstained bodies marred the green of the meadow. Neal scanned the tree line for the attackers and noticed a lone woman with brunette hair creep into the open. She took a few cautious steps then ran to a body.

"No!" She cradled the body. "Don't be dead!"

Caught up in the tragedy, Neal watched for several moments. "Come on, Ginger, it's time to leave." He slid the shotgun over his shoulder and grabbed his backpack. Before leaving, he decided to do a quick check for wounded and then hurry north. He jogged out of the trees in the direction of the nearest body.

Ten yards away the woman continued to sob.

Ginger sniffed at the corpse, but Neal didn't require a close examination. Several crimson stains marred the chest, and a nasty gash tore into the skull. Neal barely slowed before moving on. Next, he came upon a blonde woman with a single wound. He checked for a pulse but found none.

Altogether, Neal examined two men, the woman, and a boy younger than his son Drake. All were dead. None had weapons.

Neal walked to the weeping woman. Her long brunette hair hung half over her face and blood stained her clothes where she cradled the man. "Can I help?" Neal asked.

She rocked back and forth, crying softly.

Because of the closeness in age, he guessed the man was her husband. Having lost his own wife to violence, Neal understood this kind of hurt. His gut twisted in empathy. Resolving to check on her again before he left the area, Neal walked a few yards away to the cluster of corpses. Eight bodies formed a rough circle near the smoldering remains of a campfire. Ginger sniffed each body as they walked around the group. These were the leather-jacketed bikers who had strolled into the camp last night and here, in this haphazard circle, they made their last stand.

Earlier, he had noticed several with weapons, but now there were none. The speed and apparent surprise suggested a coordinated attack. The hair stood on the back of Neal's neck. The five scattered bodies were noncombatants caught in the crossfire. The gang probably had been sitting together around the fire when the attack began. They would have tried to defend themselves but barely had a chance to move before being mowed down. Who had mounted such a quick, effective attack? Neal didn't want to find out.

He jogged to the woman, still cradling the body. "I'm sorry about what happened to him, but I really think you should leave before whoever did it comes back."

For several moments she continued rocking, but then her face twisted into a wild grin. She looked toward Neal with blank, expressionless eyes and laughed, long and low.

Neal pulled on Ginger's leash and silently backed away. Had grief led to insanity or was her mind already rattled? He pulled again on the leash, turned, and jogged north toward the forest edge. There he stopped when he heard a now unusual noise—vehicles.

Several military trucks, pickups, and vans rolled to a sudden stop along two sides of the area. Men, most in uniform but some without, poured into the meadow.

"Halt! Put your hands up!"

* * *

Chelan County, Washington, Tuesday, September 6th

"You want the bike, you can have it." Conner eased away from the man.

"Oh, I want it. That backpack looks nice, too, and your jacket. Ease that rifle off your shoulder and lower it to the ground. Then take off your jacket and step away."

Still trying to decide what to do, Conner raised one hand toward the rifle and took another step back.

"If you don't do nothing stupid, you might live." The man waved the pistol. "Come on, hurry up. I don't have all day." His eyes focused on something near Conner. "Is that another bike? Is there someone else?" He glanced from side-to-side.

"No, I'm the only one here." Conner hoped Madison wouldn't return.

"You're lying."

Madison rose from the grass behind the thief and wound her arm like a windmill.

He shook the pistol at Conner. "I should kill—"

Thud.

Something bounced off the back of the man's head and he dropped to the ground.

Conner rushed to him and grabbed the pistol. Beside the man was a bloodstained rock.

Backing away, Conner stared at Madison.

"Did I kill him?" She stepped forward. When she got close enough to see the man, she gasped. "I didn't mean to kill him."

Using two fingers, Conner pressed against the man's carotid artery. He moved his fingers a couple times but found no pulse. Looking up to Madison, he smiled. "There it is. He'll have a really bad headache when he wakes up." He told her what she needed to hear. "We've got to go. He may have friends nearby."

She nodded but continued to stare.

He took her hand. "We really need to leave."

She nodded again and hurried to the campsite. They packed in haste and pedaled away fast. Conner pointed to an onramp and they continued south, weaving among abandoned cars until they left Wenatchee. Only then, when his legs demanded rest, did he ask Madison to stop.

Conner pointed to three vehicles. "It looks like the van slammed into the car and pushed it into the SUV."

She cast him a questioning look.

"I know my last hiding spot didn't work out so well, but the crash site provides good cover."

"Cover?" Madison followed him toward the wreck. "You sound like some military guy."

"I wanted to join the marines." He stopped and sighed. "Anyway, that was my plan before things fell apart. I'll check the vehicles and make sure they're empty."

Rifle ready, Conner walked around the cars, peering in the windows, and then checked the van. On the far side, he found the sliding door ajar. He yanked it open with a bang.

"Are you okay?" Madison called.

"Yeah, everything is good. Come on over."

The two sat in the entryway of the van eating their energy bar breakfast and drinking water.

"I'm lost." Madison looked down the highway. "Do you know the way back over the mountains to Olympia?"

"Sure. Well, sort of. I can get to Olympia and from there I'll need you to guide me to your house." Conner had more of a vague idea than a route traced in his mind. Go south to I-90, cross the mountains and then head south on I-5. He wished he had taken the maps in the glovebox of his truck with him, but he hadn't expected to travel across the state.

He walked to the nearest car to check for maps and anything else that might prove useful. The doors were locked. He could break the windows but decided to move on to the next vehicle. It took only a few minutes to find an unlocked car with maps. He returned to Madison and traced out the route they would take. "We'll be traveling south most of the day to Ellensburg. Then tomorrow we'll follow the freeway into the mountains."

Conner stuffed the maps and remaining food into his pack but then stopped. "When I woke this morning you were gone."

"I had to pee."

"Oh." He chuckled. "Well, thanks for taking out that guy. If you hadn't thrown that rock I might be dead now." He mimicked her toss. "Where did you learn to throw like that?"

Her face paled.

He regretted the question. "Sorry, but thank you. I mean it." He continued to pack.

After several moments, Madison stowed her few things. "Softball. I learned to throw as a pitcher for my high school team."

Conner nodded but said nothing. The two mounted their bikes and continued south toward Ellensburg and the mountains beyond.

* * *

Rural Lewis County, Washington, Tuesday, September 6th

Gruff growled low with his nose next to the front window.

Fear boiled within Drake. Early morning light poured through the front window. He should have closed the curtains. Again he berated himself for being stupid. He considered closing them now, but that would expose him to whatever, whoever, prowled outside. Gruff sniffed, growled, and barked as he stared out the window.

From his position near the couch, Drake couldn't see anything out of the norm.

Gruff barked wildly.

A dark figure dashed across the lawn.

Drake held his breath as he tried to figure out what to do. A knock at the door startled him and he fumbled with the rifle, nearly dropping it.

Gruff ran to the door barking and then wagged his tail.

Drake crept to the peephole and looked outside. "Ashley?"

"Let me in!"

He grabbed the key for the deadbolt and dropped it.

"Hurry, please!"

He searched for the key in the dark entryway. Finally, he clutched it and opened the door.

Ashley pushed her way inside, leaned against the wall, and slid down. "Shut the door." She breathed deeply. "Lock it."

*   *   *

Lebanon, Oregon, Tuesday, September 6th

Neal turned to run.

Three soldiers in camo uniforms, two privates and a major, left the cover of trees with rifles pointed at him.

Neal raised his arms.

Ginger pulled on her leash and barked wildly.

One of the privates aimed his rifle at Ginger.

"No!" Neal dropped the hand holding the leash and pulled the dog close. "We haven't done anything wrong."

"Hand over the shotgun and tie the dog to the tree," the major ordered.

Neal passed the gun to one of the soldiers and secured Ginger to a tree. Then, one of the privates frisked him and found the pistol in his jacket.

"Well, aren't you well-armed?" The major examined the pistol. "Did you kill these people?"

"No!" Neal shook his head. "Of course not. I'm just trying to get home, Major."

"Sure looked like you were trying to get away." The major waved his hand. "Come with us."

Neal fixed his gaze on the officer. "Am I under arrest?"

The major stepped close. "No, but the state is under martial law so not doing what I say could get you arrested, or shot."

As they walked away, Ginger whimpered.

"What about my dog?"

"I guess freedom for both of you depends upon your answers," the major said flatly. "Were you in the service?"

"Yes. Four years enlisted in the navy." Neal glanced at his sad dog tied to the tree. "How did you know?"

"You got my rank right."

Two soldiers led the hysterical brunette in the same direction. "No!" she shouted, looking back over her shoulder at the body of the man. She pushed one soldier and bit the other.

They threw her to the ground with a thud, yanked her wrists to her back and zip-tied them.

If the soldiers had wanted to kill him, Ginger, or the woman, they could have easily done so. While they were rough, and didn't tolerate noncompliance, Neal decided that, at least for the moment, cooperation was his best choice.

The soldiers pulled the woman to her feet. Blood flowed from her nose and lip.

As he walked toward the vehicles, he held his arms away from his body. "What do you need to know?"

The major ignored the question and turned to a nearby private. "If he tries to escape, stop him but try not to kill him. I want answers."

"Yes, sir." The private saluted.

The major walked toward a couple of police officers.

The soldiers took Neal to the convoy. From inside the nearest truck, he heard the crazy woman laugh.

* * *

Kittitas County, Washington, Tuesday, September 6th

Conner and Madison biked south along a state highway that followed the Columbia River. After several hours, they lost sight of the water as the road climbed into nearby hills.

When they stopped for a rest in the early afternoon, Conner checked the map. "We're heading southwest. I think we can be in Ellensburg by this evening."

Madison grinned and then twitched her nose. "Is that smoke I smell?"

Conner sniffed and searched the sky. "Yeah, but I can't tell where it's coming from."

They continued south and west until clouds of dark smoke hung heavy in the air, stinging Conner's nostrils and leaving an acrid taste in his mouth. Madison led by several hundred yards, but he wished she would slow down. Clearly they were traveling toward the fire. He wanted to find another route, and his legs throbbed from pedaling.

Wondering if it might be time for a break, Conner glanced at his wrist and then remembered that he had bartered his watch with Randolph in return for the bike pump. Clouds, ranging from black and smoky to white and billowy, made it difficult to gauge time by the sun.

Ahead, Madison had stopped and dismounted in the middle of the road. That wasn't the best place to rest, but he'd take any break available. Winds buffeted Conner as he climbed the hill to her side. Smoke brought tears to his eyes, making it difficult to see and more difficult to comprehend the sight. A towering wall of orange and red flame burned from the farmlands in the south toward them. Two dust devils of fire danced across the hills between them and the blazing wall.

Rabbits, deer, elk, foxes and coyotes raced from the dust and smoke past Conner and Madison.

"This way!" Conner pointed to a side road heading north.

She nodded and then pedaled off into the rolling clouds of smoke.

Despite the aching in his legs, Conner pedaled fast, trying to catch up with Madison. With each turn of the pedals, he fought to breathe the smoke-filled air into his lungs.

When the winds shifted, Conner caught an occasional glimpse of Madison. Each time she was farther ahead and the glimpse more fleeting. Once he thought he spotted her looking back at him but then lost sight of her in the smoke and dust.

Afraid he might be lost, Conner paused and looked at his map. The road ran straight for two miles, but then they needed to turn west. He had no way to tell Madison.

He pedaled hard and called her name. The smoke grated like sand within him. A gulp of water from his canteen cleansed his throat and he continued to pedal and shout for Madison. After a few minutes, he stopped by a road sign, pulled a t-shirt from his pack, dampened it with water, and tied it around his face. Then he gazed at the map, trying to determine his location.

A bike raced out of the smoke and nearly hit him.

"Madison," he croaked with a hoarse voice.

She turned back to him. "I was afraid we'd missed each other."

"No." Conner shook his head and then drank deeply. "I'm just slower than you. My legs are sore and this bike is . . ."

An ember drifted to the ground and caught nearby grass on fire.

"We can't stop here." Madison mounted her bike. "Which way do we go?"

"There's an intersection up ahead." Conner pointed along the road.

"I was just there. Follow me."

"That's seems to be all I can do—follow," Conner grumbled as she raced ahead.

Together they turned at the intersection and for more than an hour they headed west. Madison led but remained closer, never disappearing into the dark clouds. As they approached Ellensburg, she slowed and Conner rode alongside.

"I'm sorry about leaving you behind earlier."

"Lousy bike." *And flabby legs.* Conner wanted rest. "Do you have a towel or shirt we can use to make a mask for your face?"

Madison grinned. "Yeah, that would be good." They stopped and she pulled a towel from her bag.

About a mile ahead the road sloped downward. They drank and coasted into town.

"The wind seems to be blowing north."

She nodded.

"If we keep heading toward the mountains, we should veer away from the fire."

They cruised to the bottom of the slope and pedaled up the next. The top provided a vista of the surrounding city. Dark, smoky clouds filled the sky, but the town seemed untouched, at least for now. Throngs of refugees lined the road, pushing west toward the mountains. Most were on foot; some rode bikes. The eyes of most stared at the pavement.

One man drove his riding lawn mower with a woman and children in the trailer behind.

An old pickup truck, burdened with more than a dozen people, sped past.

Madison looked to Conner. "A vehicle that works?"

Conner shrugged.

Together they joined the multitude fleeing the oncoming firestorm.

Many adults seemed dazed as they left the city. An old woman with blank eyes sat in a shopping cart as a man about the same age pushed. Children and babies coughed and cried. Families held each other close as together they raced ahead of the flames.

Just west of town, the lines of refugees converged onto the freeway as it rose into the mountains. Within the mass of people, Conner found it difficult to bike. Eventually, he and Madison both dismounted and walked.

Behind him an explosion thundered.

Screams rippled through the refugees. Some ran; most trudged onward.

Conner turned. An orange ball of flame rose into the sky. Had the flames reached a fuel storage area in Ellensburg?

As the sun dipped below the western mountains, Conner slowed his pace and held out his arms. "Feel the wind?"

Madison nodded. "It changed direction."

He pointed to a nearby hill. "Let's go there."

They climbed a rocky hillside and watched the city of Ellensburg burn.

* * *

Rural Lewis County, Washington, Tuesday, September 6th

Fear grew in Drake as he stared at Ashley on the floor. Sweat rolled down her face. Again Drake fumbled with the key but managed to secure the door. "What happened?"

"Three guys with guns." Ashley struggled to breathe. "They were breaking into homes and stealing. When I heard shots, I ran."

"Did they see you?" Drake peered out the window with his rifle ready. "Did they follow you?"

"No. I don't think so."

Drake relaxed a bit. He wanted to remind her that he had said she should stay with him but thought better of it. "You can stay here as long as you want."

"Do you think someone got shot? Maybe they're hurt or dead?" She curled into a ball and cried. "What's happened to my mom and dad? What's happening to … to everywhere?"

Gruff licked her cheek as Drake slid down beside her. In the still dimly lit hallway, he shared what little he knew about the growing crisis.

Ashley shook her head. "A storm on the sun caused all of this?"

"That's what the pastor said and his son seemed to believe it too."

"How could that be?"

He shrugged. "It's daylight so I'm going to get the electricity on."

Ashley cast him a skeptical glance. "How?"

Drake grinned and strode to the garage with Ashley following. There he grabbed a gas can and rolled the generator outside. He tried to look confident as he followed the step-by-step instructions his father had written, but as he yanked the starter cord, visions of sparks and fire surged in his mind.

The generator hummed; lights flickered on.

"The water is still cold, but in about an hour you can take a hot shower if you like."

Ashley smiled. "Really?"

He nodded. "I've got to feed the animals."

Ashley followed him, staying closer than Gruff. Inside the barn, she helped him feed the rabbits and chickens and then stayed there watching them while he milked the goats."

Later, Drake sat at the head of the dining room table, eating peanut butter and jelly sandwiches for lunch. Ashley walked in with a towel around her head and wearing his robe. Drake tried to think of something witty to say but couldn't. "I made you a sandwich."

"Thanks." She sat beside him. "Do you think the robbers are still near my house?"

"Maybe, but they probably took whatever they wanted and left."

"Would you mind if I stayed here awhile?"

Drake grinned. "Sure, I guess that would be okay." *Yes!*

She nodded and stared at her food for several moments. "I need to go back and leave a note for Mom and Dad. Also, I'll need clothes and stuff—if you think it's safe."

No, it wasn't safe. The looters might still be in the area, waiting for darkness and a chance to break into more houses. Drake recalled a comment from the orange binder about keeping weapons on each person or quickly available. He turned to Ashley. "If we go back to your house, you should have a gun."

Wide-eyed, she shook her head.

He started to insist, but if he argued with her, she might leave and go home without him. He wanted her to stay with him for good reasons … and bad. At the very least she could help keep an eye on things and might assist with chores. For now, he wouldn't argue with her about carrying a gun. "Okay." He nodded and slung the rifle over one shoulder. "Let's do this while it's still light."

* * *

Lane County, Oregon, Tuesday, September 6th

For nearly an hour, Neal sat leaning against a tire under the watchful eye of an M4-toting private. Then another soldier approached. "Where's the prisoner's backpack?"

Neal grunted at being called a prisoner.

The guard pointed to a lone backpack near a pile of other gear collected by the soldiers.

In the truck behind him, the crazy woman cackled.

The new soldier opened Neal's bag and poured the contents onto the ground, spilling some of the dog food as he did. He then restuffed the bag, checking each item as he did. "Come with me. The major wants to see you." The soldier passed the backpack to Neal.

With a soldier on each side, Neal was escorted to the major sitting under the shade of a tree behind a portable table. Several empty chairs were positioned nearby.

The private stopped and saluted. "Sir, the prisoner had a small knife in the bag, but no other weapons or suspicious items." He passed the knife to the major.

The major examined it and set it on the table. "My name is Major Franklin." He gestured for Neal to sit in one of the empty chairs.

"Neal." As he sat, the chair rocked on the uneven ground. "Ah, Neal Evans."

Major Franklin nodded slowly and then continued. "Since the solar storm, we've had problems with looters and the general criminal element. We've had a particularly bad time with one militia group that has been raiding and killing in this area."

"I have nothing to do with them or what happened here."

"I don't think you do either, but somehow everyone else in that park ended up dead or crazy." He leaned forward. "So, tell me what happened. Who was in the park when you arrived?"

"Thirty, maybe forty, men, women, and children."

"Were they armed? Did there appear to be any military organization?"

"No. They seemed like a bunch of refugees."

The major wrote on a pad. "Go on."

"Later, eight men came into the meadow. They looked like a biker gang, minus the bikes. I thought they would be a problem."

"Where were you when they arrived?"

"In the trees just to the west." Neal pointed to where he had camped. "Anyway, after a while things settled down, and I fell asleep. Just before dawn, rapid gunfire erupted. I stayed down low until there was enough light to see."

"So, all the shooting happened while it was still dark?"

Neal nodded. "I think they must have had night vision gear. They killed the bikers in seconds. I think the other bodies in the meadow were collateral damage."

The major jotted more notes on his pad.

"Please, you've got to believe me. I'm just trying to get home. I didn't kill anyone."

"I believe you." The major slid the knife back to Neal. "Will you be going through Portland?"

"You're letting me go?"

The major nodded.

"Yeah, I'll need to go through parts of the city. I'll probably avoid the downtown area. Can you tell me what the situation is in Portland now?"

The major shook his head. "I wish I knew. My family lives there." For the next couple of minutes, he wrote. Then he sealed each of two pages in its own envelope and wrote on the covers. Holding one up, he said, "This is for my commanding officer in Portland. If you make it there, I've asked him to provide you safe passage through the city."

"Thank you. Who is the other letter for?"

"My wife and children. Please let them know that I'm okay."

* * *

Kittitas County, Washington, Tuesday, September 6th

"The fire is moving north." Conner pointed to his left. "If it keeps moving that way, we should be safe. We can stay here for a while."

Madison nodded.

He dropped his backpack and sat, grateful that she had agreed. Smoke still hung heavy in the air, and the fire would destroy much of Ellensburg by morning, but he didn't think he could pedal any farther.

She sat beside him. "It'll be dark soon. Do you want to camp here for the night?"

"That might be a good idea." He massaged his sore legs.

While the long line of refugees continued up both sides of the freeway into the mountains, several small groups broke off and joined Conner and Madison on the hill.

A family with two teen girls and a younger boy struggled to the summit. Each carried at least one cloth bag stuffed with possessions. Another man and woman huddled nearby. Somewhere in the growing darkness, a baby cried.

It would get cold up on the hill, but the breeze kept the air clearer. Conner had breathed enough smoke and seen enough flames for a lifetime. He pulled out two energy bars from his backpack and passed one to Madison. "That's the last of the food."

A woman cradling a baby climbed to the top of the hill.

Madison ate quickly and then stared at the wrapper. "Thanks."

"For what?"

"Sharing your food with me."

"You saved my life this morning. We help each other." He passed the sleeping bag to her. "The best chance we have to get home is by working together."

A lone man strode up the hill.

"Let's move away from the others." Conner picked up his gear. "I don't want someone pulling a gun on me while I sleep."

Walking with the bikes and gear on his back, they hiked to a more secluded spot a few hundred yards away.

"There are so many people in the area, someone should stay awake." Conner set his bike against a tree. "I'll take—."

"No." Madison tossed him the sleeping bag. "I'll stay awake. You had a rougher day biking than I did. Get some sleep."

Conner started to protest, but Madison pointed to the sleeping bag. "You first."

"Okay. Wake me…." He pulled up his sleeve to check his watch and remembered he had traded it. "Wake me when you get tired." He slid into the bag and closed his eyes. Despite hunger, worry, and rocky ground, sleep snared him in seconds.

He could taste smoke on his tongue. It tickled his nose as he woke. How long had he been asleep?

"Conner, wake up. The wind changed direction."

*   *   *

Rural Lewis County, Washington, Tuesday, September 6th

Drake put Gruff on a leash, and with Ashley alongside, they headed out. The rifle seemed heavy on his shoulder and his stomach churned as they walked toward Ashley's home. Out of habit, he walked along the road edge, but no cars passed and he hoped they wouldn't encounter any looters.

Pastor Wayne waved from the porch as they neared his house. "Glad to see you're okay, Drake. Did you hear the shooting this morning?"

"No, I slept through it." As Drake walked over to the front porch, he noticed a shotgun beside the old man. Drake introduced Ashley. "We're going to get stuff from her house."

"Mind if I walk with you?" Before Drake could answer, Wayne stood and grabbed the shotgun. "It'll do me good to stretch my legs and look around the neighborhood." He hurried down from the porch and petted Gruff.

As they continued toward Ashley's house, Drake glanced at the older man. "It seems strange to see a preacher walking around with a shotgun."

"I did four years in the marines before I was a pastor and I've done a fair amount of hunting." He looked Drake up and down. "It seems strange to see a teenager walking down the road with a rifle over his shoulder." Wayne grinned.

When they arrived at Ashley's home, she retrieved a key from a nearby flower pot, but before she unlocked the door, Wayne waved for her to stop. "I'll check around back. You two stay here. Holler if anyone suspicious comes around." Leading with the shotgun, he disappeared around the corner of the house.

Drake swept his gaze along the street. All the nearby homes seemed quiet or deserted, but farther down the road, Drake spotted a broken window and an open front door. Gruff idly sniffed the ground.

Pastor Wayne returned moments later. "Everything is secure in back. Unlock the door and I'll do a quick check inside. Both of you keep watch out here." He stepped inside and returned a few minutes later. "Okay, Ashley, get what you need and let's leave before the sun sets."

Drake nodded agreement.

Ashley dashed through the open door and up the stairs.

After a few moments, Pastor Wayne turned to Drake. "Yesterday you said that your father was home, but that's not true, is it?"

Drake felt his face flush. "No. I'm not sure where he is, or my brother."

"Hopefully they'll show up soon, but until then the best thing would be for you two to come and stay at my place. We already have three families in our house, but we can manage."

"No." Ashley stepped onto the porch with a suitcase. "I don't know you, but I know Drake. My parents said I could go to his house. I'll stay with him till they come back." She set the case down by Drake.

Wayne started to say something, but Ashley shook her head and disappeared into the house again.

"I'm staying on the farm," Drake said with equal finality. "There are enough supplies to last us for a while and I need to take care of the animals."

Pastor Wayne stared at Drake with a serious expression, and then his face softened. "Ecclesiastes tells us there is a time for everything. I guess this is the time a boy becomes a man."

Drake grinned at being called a man.

Wayne's face returned to a more serious composure. "But you aren't grown yet and I need to speak with you like a parent would." He took a deep breath. "Clearly, Ashley trusts you. You need to honor that trust and be a gentleman. Your mother and father would expect that of you. You protect her and don't use or hurt her. Do you understand what I'm telling you?"

Drake felt like the pastor had smacked him in the face. Adults sure knew how to play the guilt trip. "Yes, I understand."

Moments later Ashley returned with a second suitcase and a school backpack. "I left a note for my parents."

Drake and the pastor each grabbed a case and the three hurried away from the empty house as the sun disappeared below the trees.

Day four

Lane County, Oregon, Wednesday, September 7th

Major Franklin carefully folded the note and then slid it across the desk along with Neal's knife.

Neal stared at the address and directions and then at the major. "You're not heading north?"

The major shook his head. "The militia group we've been ordered to ... ah, neutralize seems to be moving south. Since you're heading north, I'm hoping you will pass the letter along for me. The unit established a base camp near the University of Portland."

Conflicting emotions flooded Neal. He wanted to help the major, but more than anything he wanted to get home to Drake and Conner.

"Of course, we'll return your weapons."

"I've been to the campus. I'll try to deliver your message. Can I get some food?"

"If by food you mean MREs." The major grinned. "We can spare a few."

Worried that he might change his mind, Neal stashed the three MREs the major offered into his pack and retrieved his shotgun and pistol from the guard. Then he jogged across the meadow.

When Ginger spotted him, she jumped to her feet and barked excitedly.

"Yeah, girl, I'm free and you'll be in a second." He untied her while she licked his face and then they hurried out of Lebanon.

Neal avoided Albany and hiked along the quieter rural roads. He soon crossed the South Santiam River and later in the day crossed the north fork. Along the way he saw many dark homes and the occasional barking dog, but no other refugees passed as he continued his northward trek.

Only when the darkness became so deep that he had trouble following the road did he stop and sleep in a grove of trees.

Neal awoke to dog breath. As his eyes crept open, Ginger licked his face. "Okay, okay, I'm awake." Neal pushed the dog back, sat up, and wiped his face. He felt the stubble of his growing beard and imagined he looked like a bum. He slid from the sleeping bag, pulled off his shoes and socks, and rubbed his sore feet. Taking a knife, he popped a few blisters.

Four days. That was all the time necessary to transform him from a well-paid financial planner into a homeless beggar sleeping under a canopy of trees. His former life seemed like a half-forgotten dream.

Neal stood and rubbed his sore back and legs. Perhaps he should stay and rest here today. He leaned against a tree and slid to the ground. "Let's get some breakfast, girl."

Ginger wagged her tail.

He fed the dog and then opened an MRE for himself. Nearby a small creek babbled through a culvert under the road. He should rest here for a while more. He slumped to prone position and napped.

It seemed only minutes later that Ginger whined in Neal's ear. Startled from a dream, he flailed his arms, sat up, and opened his eyes. He was tired, sore, and *really* wanted a cup of coffee.

Over a hundred miles of hiking remained ahead of him. His feet still hurt. Even with the MREs, he would run out of food before reaching home. Were Drake and Conner okay? Were they alive?

Ginger nudged him.

"You're right, girl, I need to get off my butt and head home." He stood, packed his gear, and continued north.

Determination remained tempered by pain in a multitude of places and slowed his pace. Several hours passed before whiffs of smoke hinted that Salem might be near. The road he hiked along widened from two to four lanes and more side roads intersected it.

Neal didn't want to go through the town and began searching for a way around. He turned east and then onto a two-lane road that paralleled the freeway.

As he hiked north past farms and fields, the smell of noxious smoke increased. A few hundred yards along, the road climbed, causing him to slow. When he reached the crest, thin lines of black smoke swirled into the air beyond a cluster of splintered trees.

What could have broken and charred the trees? The foul smoke caused him to gag. This wasn't burning trees. Something else smoldered just out of view.

Now curious, Neal jogged toward the next bend in the road.

The noxious smoke increasingly irritated his nose and mouth as he rounded a bend and came to a long straight stretch of road. Neal halted and stared. In the field ahead lay the shattered and charred wreckage of a commercial airplane.

* * *

Kittitas County, Washington, Wednesday, September 7th

"Wake up," Madison repeated. "The fire is coming this way."

Conner bolted to his feet. Most of the world remained dark, but to the east devilish fingers of fire burned toward him along both sides of the freeway.

Shouts and screams mixed with the crackle of flames. Below Conner, hundreds of shadow-like figures ran west along the highway. Some who couldn't run faster than the flames veered off and plunged into the nearby Yakima River.

"Pack," Madison commanded as she tossed her bag over a shoulder.

Conner nodded and stuffed gear into his bags.

Madison grabbed her bike but waited nearby until Conner finished packing. Then they both dashed down the slope toward the freeway. Conner struggled to catch up with Madison but couldn't, so he mounted his bike and, like a skier, flew down the slope. Careening down the hill, Conner caught up with Madison. Then his bike hit a bump that flung him into the air. Hitting the ground with a thud, he rolled to a stop in the dirt.

"Are you okay?" From a few yards ahead, Madison looked back at him with wide, frightened eyes.

The crackle of fire mixed with the screams of women and men.

"Yes! Go on! I'll catch up." Conner raced back only to discover a bent and mangled wheel. He tossed aside the now useless bike but kept the pump thinking Madison might use it. Then he rushed down the hill after her with only a few yards between him and flame.

Screams hung in the air with the smoke and ash.

Finding no sign of Madison, he sprinted west along the freeway and up the slope.

Coughing and wheezing from the foul air, Conner ran past two elderly couples and several parents with small children in their arms and on their backs. Would they be able to stay ahead of the flames? He didn't know, and had no idea how he might help them. *Please God, keep them safe.*

Catching a second wind, Conner scrambled up to the crest of the next hill. There a cool breeze swept his sweaty face. The wind had changed direction again. He looked back at flames now hundreds of yards behind him and drawing no closer. Hoping to put much more distance between him and fiery death, Conner continued running until he gasped for air. Then he slowed to a jog and eventually walked.

In the growing pre-dawn light, he spotted a cliff. He jogged from the freeway, climbed through the trees to the rocky outcrop, and stood near the edge of the cliff looking over thousands of acres of forest and flame. No humans would come and fight this fire. How long would it burn? Would it continue to scorch the Earth until the fall rains?

He looked at the freeway. Like a line of ants, hundreds weaved west. Was Madison in that line? Was she okay? Would he be able to find her?

* * *

Rural Lewis County, Washington, Wednesday, September 7th

Sunlight flowed through open curtains, waking Drake. After dressing, he grabbed the rifle by his bed and walked the few steps to his brother's room, where Ashley slept. He thought about knocking but decided to let her sleep. With Gruff at his side, he left to feed the animals, including the Hamiltons' horses, and milked the goat.

Clouds obscured the sun and the morning breeze felt cool. Thankfully, the animals had enough water, saving him the chore of hand pumping.

Within thirty minutes, Gruff and Drake had both finished what they had to do and returned to the house.

Ashley stood in the kitchen, wearing a pastel blue robe. She rubbed her eyes. "Have you had breakfast?"

"No, not yet."

She opened the refrigerator. "I'll cook eggs and bacon if you start the generator, but then I'd *really* like a hot shower."

Anything you want. "Sure."

She held a green egg in one hand and a blue one in the other. "Are these chicken eggs?"

"Yes. Ready for Easter." Drake grinned "Just kidding. That's how some chickens lay them. They're normal inside." The smile lingered as he strode toward the garage to start the generator. He used the last fuel from one of the gas cans to fill the tank. How long would the gas last even if they only used the generator a few hours each day? Could he find more fuel somewhere?

Drake fired up the generator. At least for a while, Ashley would have hot showers and he wouldn't have to pump water for the animals.

Ashley set a plate of bacon, eggs, and crackers in front of Drake. He held one of the crackers, staring at it. "Why did you add these?"

"We're out of bread. There're boxes of them in the pantry."

"Really? Boxes?" Drake smeared jam on one. It would do fine. He took another bite. The food, the fuel, the generator; even the animals and fruit trees, all of it had been his father's idea, but he had never appreciated it. *Thanks Dad. Come home quick, please.*

"I was going to ask about the heaters, but I think I know the answer."

Drake looked out the window. "The clouds are thinning. It should warm up later this morning. I don't want to use the electric heaters for that—not yet anyway."

"What about the wood stove?"

For several moments, Drake pondered the question. The smoke would reveal that someone lived in the house, but would that knowledge keep looters away or encourage them. Ashley had said that looters were near her house, not very far away, and that someone had been shooting.

His dad would have an answer, but he had none, and decided to put off the decision. "Let's not use the woodstove yet."

Ashley frowned. "I'll get a sweater."

All the problems that harassed his mind and troubled his sleep drove Drake back to his father's office and the folders that now provided the only insight he had to his dad's thoughts. While he read, Gruff curled up nearby.

Several hours later, Ashley, now dressed in jeans and a purple shirt, strolled into the office, carrying a tray. "You look like an executive behind that desk."

"I feel like a student." He set the folder down. "Is that tray for me?"

"Yes." She placed it in front of him. "Water, crackers with cheese, and some apple slices. It's not much, but I thought you'd be getting hungry. I was going to give you cereal for lunch, but the milk tasted funny so I poured it out."

Drake felt annoyed but ended up grinning.

"What did I do?"

"The milk tasted funny because it was goat's milk."

"You actually drink it?"

"And use it on cereal." He hoped they would be together long enough for her to grow used to it. "If any does go bad, we can still feed it to the animals, so don't throw it out."

Ashley set the tray on the desk with a frown.

"Thanks," Drake said and watched her behind sway on her way out of the room. Having Ashley here was really good, but he worried about their future. Gas would run low in a couple of weeks. Food for the animals wouldn't last the month. How long would the human food last? He didn't know. His father had stocked the pantry and more had been stored in the survival room, but, even if only he and Ashley ate it, the food would eventually run out.

When he finished lunch, he closed the folder, grabbed the tray, and walked toward the kitchen with Gruff.

Ashley hurried around a corner and slammed into Drake.

"What's the hurry?"

Her eyes were wide with fear. "Two men are in the backyard."

* * *

Lane County, Oregon, Wednesday, September 7th

Neal tugged on Ginger's leash, but the dog found sniffing the air and ground more compelling. Had the plane carried passengers? Is death what Ginger smelled? Images of burned and mangled bodies flashed through Neal's mind. Trying to avoid such sights and smells, Neal pulled hard on the leash, nearly dragging the dog as he hurried in an arc around the largest portion of the smoldering plane. Then he scurried across a wide cut in the ground where the craft had apparently belly-flopped in the pasture. From there it seemed to have skidded, plowed deeper into the ground, and broken apart.

In normal times there would have been a huge police and first responder presence. No one just hiking by could have ventured this close without crossing police tape and being ordered away, but in a mere four days, the world had changed.

On the far side of the wreckage, hundreds of postal packages lay strewn across the field. A few large crates had broken open, spilling boxes of computers and televisions beside the shattered fuselage. Neal stopped and stared with the sudden realization that this had been a mail and cargo flight. The crew were probably dead somewhere in the wreckage, but at least there hadn't been hundreds of passengers. He crept through the debris wondering how many planes had crashed on the night of the EMP. How many people had died?

Ahead, a child-like form lay motionless on the ground.

Neal feared what he would find but felt compelled to confirm what his eyes told him. He brushed away paper and packages and grinned with relief. Grabbing it by an arm, he picked up the life-size infant doll.

"Mommy."

The voice startled him even though he knew it came from a toy.

Ginger clamped her teeth on one leg of the doll and shook it.

"Get away from that stuff!" The voice shouted from behind.

"I'm not taking anything." Neal eased himself to a standing position and, with his arms away from his body, slowly turned to face the new threat.

Ginger dropped the doll and growled.

Ten yards away stood a wrinkled, gray-haired man with a ball cap on his head and a pistol in his hand. A few feet behind the old guy stood a woman with salt-and-pepper hair wearing faded jeans.

"The plane crashed on my land," the old guy yelled. "This is all my stuff."

Neal had a shotgun over his shoulder and a pistol in his vest but decided to back away. "Just passing through. Come on, Ginger, let's go." Keeping his arms away from his torso, he tugged on the leash and eased toward the road. Then he hurried to put some distance between them.

When he looked back and couldn't see the wreck, he considered slowing his pace but rejected it. If he stayed out of Salem and walked all night, he might reach Portland by tomorrow morning.

I'm coming, boys. Please stay safe.

* * *

Kittitas County, Washington, Wednesday, September 7th

Conner returned to the highway and tried to concentrate on the hike home. He had left his little brother alone. The guilt of that beat in his brain like a mantra. He tried to focus on just the route home, but traversing that would still take days and seemed overwhelming.

The climb to Snoqualmie Pass would take more than a day, but after that the trip would be largely downhill into Seattle. He narrowed in on just that portion of the route, but even then he found his mind drifting. Where was Madison? Would she be okay? They spent less than two days together, but even after so little time her image lingered in his mind. Would he ever see her again?

She had a bike and stamina and might now be miles ahead. If he were to ever find her, he would need to catch up. He strode onward and soon reached the trailing edge of refugees from Ellensburg. Madison had worn a pastel blue and white jacket so every relatively blue coat caught his attention, but those within view were worn by elderly or infirm walkers.

Just ahead, a significantly overweight man and woman tried to keep up with several rambunctious children. On his right, a group helped a young man on crutches hobble along. Nearby, a middle-age man pushed a wheelchair that carried an old woman. Most of those nearby seemed past retirement age with gray hair. Could these people make it over the mountain and reach help? Would there be any help?

He slowed his pace and looked again at those around him. They all might be dead in the next few weeks.

"Martha, are you okay?" a panicked elderly voice called. "Talk to me."

An old man with thin white hair slumped to the shoulder of the road, holding a woman about his age.

Conner hurried over as the man cradled her head in his lap.

"We'll rest. You'll be better." The man tearfully stroked her shoulder-length hair. "Please be okay."

"I'm Conner. Is she okay?"

He shook his head.

"May I check her pulse?"

He nodded. "Are you a doctor?" The words were both a question and a plea.

"No." Conner shook his head. "I know first aid." He checked both her neck and wrist without finding a pulse.

"Do you know CPR?" the old man asked.

"Yes."

For an exhausting fifteen minutes, Conner performed chest compressions while the man breathed for the woman, but she never responded.

The old man slumped back and clutched her hand. "She won't be waking up. You should stop. Her heart was weak. Let her rest."

Conner wiped sweat from his forehead. "Ah, if we do …."

The old man nodded and looked to the sky. "She's in Your hands now, Lord. Take good care of her." He kissed her cheek.

For several minutes, Conner sat in silence, trying to think of what to do or say. He had seen more death in the last four days than in all his life. This had been the most peaceful, but he didn't think that would be the right thing to say.

"Your name's Conner, right? Mine is Arthur. Thank you for your help."

Conner nodded, uncertain what help he had provided.

"We have family in Seattle, a son, a couple of grandchildren and great-grandchildren. We were trying to reach them."

"I left my little brother alone the day before the sun storm. Now I'm trying to get back home to Riverbank."

Arthur nodded but said nothing.

Conner felt a need to talk and so continued his story of meeting Madison, passing through Ellensburg, and then losing her after crashing his bike.

Arthur caressed Martha's hand. "We married right out of high school and had our first boy a year later." Tears rolled down his cheeks. "I enlisted in the marines and served for eight years. Then we moved back here and have been together more than sixty years."

"I've been trying to figure out how to tell my dad I wanted to join the marines. I guess that doesn't matter anymore."

He smiled at Conner. "You're a good young man, and you would have made a great marine. Your parents raised you right. No matter how ugly this world gets, remember the things they taught you."

Again they sat in silence.

"I can't leave her here alone."

"What choice do you have? We don't have the tools to bury her."

"There's always a choice, young man. Help me get her out of the road."

When they had moved her to a shady spot nearby, Conner asked, "What are you going to do now?"

"I'm going to stay with Martha."

"No one will come. No police, no ambulance."

"I'm eighty-five. In this new world where nothing works, how long do you think I'd live?"

"I don't know."

"I think you do." He pulled a plastic bag with half a dozen pill bottles from the luggage. "These were Martha's. I guess now they're mine." He smiled at Conner. "Thank you for your help. I'm staying with my wife."

"I'm sorry I couldn't have been more help." Conner lingered, feeling torn between staying to help and continuing his own odyssey home.

After a moment, Arthur turned to Conner. "You should find that young lady you were talking about."

They shook hands and Conner left, still trying to decide if he should have stayed and tried harder to convince Arthur to go on to Seattle. Would Arthur have been able to survive the trip?

For the rest of the day, Conner continued his trek into the mountains. As the sun slid below a nearby peak, a church bell echoed through the growing darkness. Hungry and thirsty, he entered the small town of Cle Elum.

*   *   *

Rural Lewis County, Washington, Wednesday, September 7th

Drake slid the rifle from his shoulder and held it in his hands while trying to decide what to do. He stepped close to a back window. "I don't recognize either of them."

Both were older than his father; one was overweight, the other skinny by comparison. They both wore faded jeans, heavy boots, and several days of salt-and-pepper stubble. If he had seen them along the road, he would have thought they were homeless.

The two pumped water from the well and drank, stared at the horses, chickens and goats, and walked among the apple trees still burdened with fruit.

"What are we going to do?" Ashley whispered.

"I don't know." Drake didn't want to confront them; they hadn't done any harm. "For now let's just watch."

While Drake gazed out the window, Gruff pranced back and forth, sniffing the air. With a low growl, he scurried across the kitchen and out the doggy door.

The man closest to the house, the skinny one, pulled a pistol from his pocket.

Drake ran out the door with his rifle ready. "Don't shoot my dog! Gruff, come!"

Gruff stopped midway between Drake and the man.

Skinny pointed his weapon but didn't fire.

"Gruff, come." Drake stepped forward.

"Hey kid, where's your dad?" Skinny asked.

Why did everyone want to know that? "He's coming. You better leave."

"Sure kid, or maybe I could talk with him."

Gruff growled.

Drake shook his head at Skinny and called for Gruff again. His jaw clinched and anger grew as Gruff ignored him and continued growling.

"Is that your sister?" Skinny asked.

Gruff eased forward with a low growl.

A glance over Drake's shoulder revealed Ashley standing on the back steps. The thought of using the stay command on Ashley flashed through his mind.

"She's kinda cute," Fatty said. "What's your name, girl?"

"You two need to leave." Drake struggled to keep his voice steady.

"I'm going to kill that dog if it gets any closer." Skinny thrust the pistol in Gruff's direction.

Fatty grinned at Ashley. "Come to papa."

A startled look on Fatty's face caused Drake to glance over his shoulder.

Ashley ran past Drake toward Fatty, but she stopped at Gruff, grabbed his collar, and pulled the dog back to the steps.

Relieved that Ashley was out of the way, Drake returned his attention to the men. "Leave," he said with as much menace as he could muster.

Skinny smiled. "Okay, kid. I'll speak with your dad—later."

Drake felt his face flush with anger at the two men and at Ashley. Why had she left the house? Why had she rushed across the yard and grabbed Gruff?

Drake watched as the two men casually walked around the house and back toward the road.

As Drake stepped inside, he slid in the metal plate, closing the doggy door. Ashley waited in the dining room, still holding onto Gruff.

"Are they gone?" she asked.

"Yes. For now." Drake cleared the chamber and leaned the gun into a corner. "I'm mad at both of you."

"Me? And Gruff?"

"Yes." He stepped closer to Ashley. "Why did you go outside?"

She stood and planted both hands on her hips. "You went out first."

"I'm a guy. I had a gun."

"What has you being a guy got to do with anything?"

"Ah … well, guys are supposed to protect girls."

Ashley grinned. "Where's your shiny armor?"

"Huh?"

"Thank you. I didn't want that guy to hurt you or Gruff."

Drake's face still burned. "Gruff needs serious obedience training."

She stuck out her lower lip in a pout. "Don't be mad. I just wanted them to go away."

"You may have given them more reason to return." The pouty face melted Drake's anger. "Keep the doors locked and stay inside today."

Drake grabbed the rifle and hurried off to the survival room. He feared the two men would return and he needed to be ready. He selected an AR-15 with a scope and found a night vision monocular on a tripod. Years ago on a dark, moonless night, he had watched his father use it.

"Two coyotes are over there," his dad had said. "That's why our animals are restless."

Drake had looked across the yard into thick blackness. Then his dad motioned for him to use the monocular. The predators at the edge of the forest came into clear view.

That night his dad had dealt with the coyotes. Tonight he expected other predators to slink onto the property.

Please Dad, come home soon.

Day five

Lane County, Oregon, Thursday, September 8th

Sore feet and exhaustion prevented Neal from hiking through the night, but the growing number of suburban homes and businesses he had seen told him he wasn't far from Portland. He had slept in the back of a looted antique store and now the light of dawn woke him from his slumber on several old rugs.

Why loot antiques? He had no answer, but the floor coverings had provided a bed for him and Ginger during the night.

Later in the day, after they reached Portland, he hoped to find a car with keys still in it. He would get it running and drive home. But before he could leave Portland, he had to reach the city and accomplish two missions.

He fed Ginger some dog food and then pulled an MRE from his pack. By that time Ginger had gulped down her food and came sniffing at his.

He pulled his food away from her. "This is mine. You've got more to eat than I do. In a couple of days, I might be sniffing at your dog food."

As he walked from the antique shop, Neal checked a nearby car for keys but found none. He tossed the MRE package into the back seat. "Come on, girl. We've got a long walk to Portland."

Neal followed the road north. Few people were going his direction, but an increasing number were heading south. Their somber exodus made him curious about conditions ahead. Just before noon, he stopped at a makeshift camp around a small pond. As Neal walked toward the water, the people watched him, and he watched them. Most of the campers appeared to be families with children. They seemed harmless, but he still positioned himself so that he could keep an eye on most of them. He filled his water bottles as Ginger lapped up mouthfuls.

A boy, about six years old, ran up to Neal. "What're you doing?"

"Getting water."

Petting Ginger, the boy said, "My daddy told me it's bad and not to drink it."

Neal nodded. "I'll filter it before I drink."

A young man ran up to the boy. "Conner, I told you not to wander off."

Neal smiled. "I have a son named Conner." He dipped his last bottle into the pond.

The young man pulled his boy close, but his face relaxed a bit. "My name is Brad. Where's home?"

"I'm Neal. I live north of here near Riverbank in Washington. Where's home for you?"

"Here for now. We used to live just outside of Portland, but a fire swept through our neighborhood."

"I'm glad you got out."

Brad nodded. "We were packed and ready. There wasn't any food or water and criminals had looted several nearby homes. The fire just made us leave a few hours earlier."

Conner's mother hurried over and took him back to their tent, but Brad stayed and continued to talk with Neal about the looting, violent crime, and lack of food.

Neal shook his head. "Ah, the good old days of peace and plenty, less than a week ago."

Brad frowned. "Last week I was a lawyer with a good firm. This week I'm a homeless bum. I hope somehow law and order is restored soon."

"You're not a bum." But Neal didn't expect normality to return soon. "I was a financial planner. Now I'm a traveler trying to reach home. How close is Portland?"

"We're just north of Wilsonville, about twelve miles from Portland. You could probably walk it in four or five hours."

"Thanks. I hope you're able to find a new home." They shook hands and Neal, with Ginger at his side, continued north.

Just after noon, Neal crested a hill where he could see the freeway stretching into Portland. Thousands of refugees hiked south along the highway out of the city. Bagpipe music reverberated from the throng. In the midst of the refugees, a fat man with thick red hair and wearing a kilt played the instrument. A hundred yards behind him, a dozen bicyclists, in various degrees of undress, pedaled along. Others chanted and sang. The smell of pot floated on the air.

Neal shook his head and stifled a grin. He would soon be in Portland.

In the distance the bang of gunfire sounded.

God, watch over my boys and speed my trip home.

*   *   *

Cle Elum, Washington, Thursday, September 8th

Conner spent the night curled in his sleeping bag in the covered entryway of Cle Elum's Catholic church. The first rays of dawn barely caused him to stir. Only when a shadow deprived him of warmth did he force open his eyes. The silhouette of a person filled his view. His arms flailed as he stumbled to his feet.

"Good morning."

"Madison?" He gazed at a bruised cheek, puffy eye, and swollen lips. "What happened to your face?"

"You sure know how to greet a girl." She grinned, but it faded quickly. "Some Neanderthal took my bike."

"Are you okay? I mean other than—"

"Other than my bruised face and pride? Yeah, I'm okay. He was more interested in the bike than me." She glanced about. "Where's your bike?"

"I bent a rim on the hill outside of Ellensburg."

"Oh, sorry, I didn't know." She stared at him for a moment. "Are you cold? Why didn't you come in?"

"The church had a guard at the door last night. He wouldn't let me in with my rifle." Conner frowned. "I wasn't going to leave it outside."

"Did you at least get some food?"

He nodded. "Yeah, a woman brought some to me."

"I'll talk with Father Dan. Yesterday evening I stumbled in here with a face full of blood and tears. He did some first aid and we talked afterward. I think he'll be reasonable. Stay here."

Madison walked inside and returned a few minutes later. "If you promise not to shoot anybody, you can come in."

"That's what Father Dan said? If I promise not to shoot anybody?"

Madison grinned and then touched her swollen lip.

"Okay, I promise." He followed her into the sanctuary crammed with people. Sweat hung heavy in the air. Many slept on the floor or in the pews; others sat or stood in clusters. Blankets, clothing, and camping gear lay scattered among the people.

Madison stopped and faced him. "I'm sorry about leaving you behind."

"You didn't know about my bike."

"I was scared. The fire. All the people running." She sighed. "I planned to stop at the pass and wait for you, but I never got there."

"I'm glad we're back together." Conner felt like hugging her but stopped at a squeeze of her hand.

A man in his early thirties strode across the room toward them. "Hi. I'm Dan." Wearing jeans and a flannel shirt, he looked more like a lumberjack than a priest. "I'm sorry about last night, but we need to be careful. Madison told me you've been helping her get home."

"We've been helping each other." Conner smiled at Madison.

"We're preparing breakfast." Dan turned and gestured. "Follow me while we talk."

The mention of food caused Conner's stomach to growl.

Dan stepped over a sleeping child. "Madison said she was from Olympia. Where's home for you, Conner?"

"On a farm just outside of Riverbank in Lewis County."

"A farm. That might be a great thing to have in the future." Dan walked in silence for several moments. "So, you'll both be heading through the Puget Sound region?"

Conner shrugged. "I guess so." He crept around a large woman sleeping on the floor.

"We're starting to see refugees from that area."

Conner shook his head. "Seattle? Tacoma? Why would they be coming this way?"

"From what I'm hearing, conditions in the metro area are bad. Most of what we've heard is from Seattle refugees, but all the news from the area is disturbing. Food is running low or already gone. Looting is rampant. Gangs control some areas. Parts of Seattle and Tacoma are burning."

Father Dan stopped and turned to them. "Are you sure you want to walk into that?"

* * *

Rural Lewis County, Washington, Thursday, September 8th

Drake awoke with a start, grabbed his AR-15 rifle from the floor in front of the couch, and looked about.

Ashley giggled as she walked across the living room toward him. "You snore."

Drake wiped his eyes. "No, I don't." Sunlight poured through the window. "What time is it?"

"Nine, I think. Do you want breakfast?"

"How long was I asleep?"

She shrugged. "You were snoring when I woke up."

"I need to feed the animals and check things before eating." Clutching the AR, Drake hurried out the backdoor. As he jogged across the yard, he yawned and rubbed heavy eyes. *I can't keep watch at night and stay awake during the day.* His foggy brain provided no solution.

As he scooped up chicken feed from the bin, Drake heard the creaking of wood. Startled, he spilled some of the food. He glanced behind him but then felt foolish. *Just the old barn creaking.* Why hadn't he brought Gruff with him?

Drake took care of the chickens and rabbits and then fed and milked the goats. As he did, an idea formed. Homes in the area had been looted. Others must have encountered such criminals. The good people of the area should cooperate. He could talk to Pastor Wayne about the idea.

He returned to the house and set the eggs and milk pail on the counter.

"Come."

Drake couldn't see Ashley, but her firm command sounded from the living room. Worried, he stepped toward her voice.

"Good boy."

Thoroughly confused, Drake peeked around the corner.

"Stay."

Ashley had Gruff on a leash.

"Come," she repeated.

"What are you doing?" Drake entered the room.

"You said Gruff needed training, and I agree. I've trained a dog before."

"You have a dog?"

She shook her head. "Not now, but I did for most of my life. I trained Lulu as part of a 4-H project." Her face lit up. "We got first place at the county fair."

"Okay." Drake didn't have the time or any idea how to train Gruff. "I hope you can do it."

She put her hands on her hips. "I can. I will."

"After breakfast, I'm going to see Pastor Wayne about Skinny and Fatty."

"Who?"

Drake explained how he had named the two thugs. "I want you to stay inside while I'm gone."

"You always want me to stay inside."

"It's safer."

"That may be true for a very long time. Do you want me to stay inside forever?"

Frustrated, Drake considered telling Ashley she could leave, but he didn't want her to go so he held back the words. "You saw those guys yesterday. It's not safe, and you won't use a gun." Drake threw up his hands. "What do you want me to say?"

She stared at him and then nodded. "I'll stay inside."

Even though Drake left Gruff with Ashley, he didn't want to be gone for long, so he hurried down the road. He expected to see Pastor Wayne on the porch, maybe even sitting with a shotgun across his lap.

He seemed like that sort of a guy. But when the porch came into view it stood empty.

Drake heard movement in the house as he walked up the steps. He knocked on the door.

All sound from within the house stopped.

*   *   *

Lane County, Oregon, Thursday, September 8th

Neal could skirt the dangers of Portland, but it would take much longer. Also, he had letters to deliver for Major Franklin. Still standing on the crest of the knoll, Neal pulled out a paper map of the Portland metro area and plotted his course into the city.

"Come on, Ginger." He stood and trod forward. "I've got a feeling today is going to be another long one."

For the next hour, Neal walked along largely empty residential streets. In the distance, an unseen child giggled. Later, a couple hurried down the opposite side of the street carrying backpacks and keeping a wary eye on him.

Ginger watched them as they passed.

Some of the homes had broken windows and doors while others seemed untouched. He tried to imagine that the parents were at work and the kids were in school. It didn't work. The hair on his neck prickled, and he could almost feel the piercing stares from dark windows.

Glass crunched under Neal's feet. He stopped. The windows of a nearby car were shattered, and the hood stood open. He shook his head, stepped back, and led Ginger around the shards. *Why break into a car that doesn't work?* As he passed, he glanced at the engine. The battery had been taken.

He turned left onto a four-lane boulevard with strip malls on either side. At the corner stood a looted gas station convenience store, with its doors hanging open and glass scattered on the pavement. Farther down the street, the windows of two fast food restaurants had been shattered. Other stores remained dark but intact.

Minutes later, Neal crested a hill that provided a long view of nearby I-5. Cars and trucks dotted the pavement, but there were no people moving along the freeway. He decided it might be safe to walk it for a while on his journey north.

He checked vehicles for keys as he hiked into the city. Three hours later, hot and tired, he still slogged along the highway. The few cars he found with keys hadn't started. He glanced in the direction of the sun, now well past its zenith. Had the storms continued? Were CMEs still hitting the Earth?

So many questions with so few answers.

Neal jogged down an off ramp and continued northwest along a wide avenue lined with trees. To the north were homes and apartments; to the south were large gray warehouses.

The breeze rustled in his ears, interrupted by occasional booms of gunfire. No planes flew overhead, no cars traveled the streets and, at least in this drab part of the city, no people ventured outside. He continued onto a wide, empty avenue toward the area Major Franklin had indicated.

Seconds later, the rumble of vehicles broke the relative silence. Surprised by the growing racket, Neal pulled Ginger onto the sidewalk as five military vehicles and a police car roared down the road. Several soldiers stared at Neal as they zipped past.

Diesel fumes hung in the air as Neal stared at his map and gazed in the direction the vehicles had gone. Were the soldiers driving to the base the major had mentioned? Did government and law still exist in the city? Did cars work? Could he get a ride home?

With Ginger at his side, Neal hurried along the boulevard in the direction the vehicles had traveled. The road twisted and bent with the river but, after nearly thirty minutes, he reached a long, gentle curve. As he rounded it, he spotted a blockade of sandbags and barbed wire.

Four men with rifles stood guard.

* * *

Rural Lewis County, Washington, Thursday, September 8th

Drake edged along the pastor's porch and glanced through the living room window. He didn't see anyone but hoped if they saw him, his look would appear nonchalant and not like someone about to break in. He returned to the door and knocked again. "Hello?"

No sound came from inside.

The voice of Pastor Wayne bellowed loud and angry from nearby. "Get out of here!"

Shaken by the harsh tone of the words that seemed directed at him, Drake stepped off the porch.

"You heard me!"

Drake retreated across the lawn but soon realized the pastor's words came from the backyard. Drake edged along the house in the direction of the voice. Turning the corner, he spotted Skinny with Pastor Wayne nearby.

Drake brought the rifle to his shoulder.

Skinny had his back to Drake, but the pastor locked eyes on him. "Don't shoot, Drake."

Skinny turned. "Boy, you seem to like pointing that gun at me. I might have to teach you a lesson."

"What are you …" Drake's voice cracked. He pressed the rifle butt hard against his shoulder and looked down the sight at Skinny's head.

Pastor Wayne stepped toward Drake but spoke to Skinny. "I think it's time for you to leave."

The back door of the house flew open. Dan, Pastor Wayne's son, hurried out holding a pistol. He wobbled the gun in Drake's direction and then at Skinny and back toward Drake.

Pastor Wayne gestured at Skinny. "Dan, aim the gun at this one."

Dan did as instructed while his face grew paler with each passing moment. Drake feared he might pass out.

"Me and my friends, we were just trying to get to know our neighbors." Skinny shook his head. "But it's clear you don't want to be friends. So, sure I'll go—for now."

Just as he had done at Drake's house, Skinny strolled away.

Dan slumped onto the back porch. "Criminals trying to break into the house, wandering around the backyard, me waving a gun … I don't know how to use a gun." His head sagged between his legs. "I can't live like this."

Drake lowered the rifle and stepped closer to the pastor. "I came to talk with you about Skinny."

"Skinny?" Pastor Wayne questioned.

"That's what I call that guy." Drake bit his lip. "He was at my house yesterday—with a friend I nicknamed Fatty. I think they were checking to see who lived there and what we had."

"Of course they were." Still slumped on the back steps, Dan lifted his head and continued. "Someone has tried to break into our home twice. We need to notify the police."

"How?" Drake asked.

Dan groaned. "I guess we need to walk into Riverbank and find the sheriff."

Drake gazed in the direction of town. "Do you think he and the deputies are still on duty?"

Wayne shook his head. "No, and even if they are, how effective could they be without cars, communications, and computers?"

Drake shrugged. "How effective were sheriffs in the Old West?"

Wayne shook his head and then stood in silence for a moment. "Skinny mentioned friends just before leaving. I've got an idea. Come into the house, and we'll discuss it."

Just inside the door, Wayne and Dan hung their jackets on a rack. An older woman with long, gray hair peeked around the corner.

"This is my wife, Mary," Wayne said with a smile. "Mary, this is Drake, Beth's son."

"I'm glad to see you again, Drake." She stepped close and squeezed his hand. "Your mother was a dear friend. We've missed you and the rest of your family. Have you been getting enough food?"

Drake smiled and nodded.

The pastor led everyone through the kitchen into a combination living and dining room.

"Over there with the baby is my daughter, Katy." Wayne nodded toward a brunette-haired woman breastfeeding an infant under a blue towel. She smiled.

Drake smiled back but, embarrassed, quickly looked away.

Wayne pulled a chair out from the dining table. "Sit here, Drake. I've got to get some things." He turned down the hall. "I'll be right back.

As he sat at the table, Drake looked around the room. He had always seen neighbors as merely people next door or down the street but now, in a time when his family was gone, these people welcomed him into their home. Pastor Wayne and his wife had shown him kindness. Afraid that tears would roll from his eyes, Drake wiped his face.

Moments later, Wayne returned with a backpack and he and Dan sat at the table with Drake.

"What's your idea, Dad?"

"I'll hike down to Riverbank and see if any law enforcement personnel are still on duty. Before we take the law into our own hands, we should check if any still exists. While I'm checking in Riverbank, you and Drake go around the community and tell people that we'll have a meeting this evening at the church."

Dan shook his head. "I should hike into town. You should walk around here with Drake."

Wayne raised an eyebrow. "Why?"

"I'm younger, I can hike faster, and everyone on Fremont Hill knows you and won't shoot at you."

"Okay." Pastor Wayne nodded. "Then Drake should go with you to Riverbank."

"No." Dan shook his head.

Pastor Wayne leaned back in his chair. "Why do you want Drake to go with me?"

"In case someone *does* shoot at you." Dan shook his head. "You have a way of finding trouble, and I'm worried you'll find it and no friend will be around."

For some reason, Drake found that idea amusing and giggled.

Wayne smiled at his son. "Okay then, we have a plan."

Drake remembered leaving Ashley at home. "Uh … what if Skinny and Fatty come back?" He had told her it would be safer at their house, but now fear boiled within him. "Ashley is alone at home, and Skinny knows I'm here." He stood and moved toward the back door as he spoke. "I've got to get home."

"I need to discuss security for this house with Mary." Wayne nodded. "Go. I'll be just a minute or two behind you."

Drake darted from Pastor Wayne's house and sprinted toward home. In a car, this part of the road had always seemed short, straight, and level, but since the sun storm, he had noticed how far away his neighbors lived. He also noticed every slope and turn. There were so many places a person could hide. As he neared his home, he slowed to a walk and tried to listen and look for movement.

Ready to run or fight, he strode around the last bend before his driveway. A hundred yards ahead, a group of six men stood talking. Drake gripped his rifle but continued toward the driveway a few feet away.

One man turned.

"Hey, kid, nice to see you again." Skinny smiled.

The other five men stared at Drake.

Fatty grinned. "How's your sister?"

Fear, both within himself and for Ashley, propelled Drake down the driveway with the rifle in his hand. Reaching the front door, he twisted the knob, but it didn't budge. He had told Ashley to lock the doors and hadn't brought his key.

Drake pounded on the door, shouted, and then listened as Gruff barked and scurried across the wood floor.

But no one unlocked the door.

"Ashley, it's me!" Drake banged again.

The deadbolt slid back with a click and the door popped open.

Drake stumbled into the house and hugged Ashley. Relief at seeing her okay and at being home flowed through him.

Gruff pushed between him and Ashley.

"What's wrong?" Ashley hugged him back. "Are you okay?"

"Yes." Drake hoped that Ashley couldn't hear his heart pounding in his chest. After a deep breath, he released her and locked the door. "I was worried about you."

"Why? You're scaring me. What happened?"

Ashley's face paled as Drake described the encounters at Pastor Wayne's home and on the road coming back to the house.

Directly behind Drake, someone knocked on the door.

Ashley gasped.

Gruff growled.

Drake spun around and leaned to the peephole. "It's Pastor Wayne." Drake let him in.

"Did you see Skinny and his cohorts?" Pastor Wayne adjusted the rifle slung on his shoulder.

"Yes." Drake nodded. "Did they give you any trouble?"

Gruff sniffed at the pastor's leg then wagged her tail.

Ashley clutched Drake's arm.

"No." Wayne shook his head. "They didn't see me. They're headed away from our homes."

Ashley sagged against the wall.

Pastor Wayne smiled at Drake. "Perhaps you should stay here with Ashley."

Drake's heart still pounded and his mouth felt dry. He wanted to stay locked in the house, but he didn't want Pastor Wayne out walking alone. He struggled to find the right thing to do.

"Pastor, what about your family?" Ashley asked. "Will they be safe?"

"I'm not sure safe is a word we can use right now. I told Dan to wait about thirty minutes before hiking into Riverbank. I wanted to make sure Skinny and any others were gone. If there was any trouble after that, I told Mary to fire the shotgun out a window and we'd come running." He shrugged. "That's about the best we can do right now."

Drake shook his head. "We can't live like this."

Ashley stared at Drake for a moment. "I'm not sure I could shoot someone, but show me how to fire the shotgun." She turned to the pastor. "I'll use it as a signal like you told Mary."

Drake left and returned with a twenty-gauge shotgun. He showed Ashley how to rack the slide and hold the weapon with the butt pressed against her shoulder.

"The gun is fully loaded, and a shell is in the chamber. The safety is off." Drake nodded toward a window. "Just point the gun out a window and pull the trigger. We'll hear it. Skinny and friends will probably scatter before we can run here."

Pastor Wayne nodded. "But if they don't leave, pump and shoot again and, if need be, at them."

Ashley stared at the gun but said nothing.

Seeing her hold the shotgun like it might bite, Drake wanted to stay with her. At the same time, Skinny, Fatty, and the others made him angry. Stay at home and protect the one he loved, or go with Pastor Wayne and help keep everyone safe.

"Are we ready to go?" Pastor Wayne asked.

The honest answer was no, but with a lingering gaze at Ashley, Drake followed Pastor Wayne out the door.

"I told Dan to knock on the doors around our house and others on the way into Riverbank." Pastor Wayne pointed toward his house. "So, we'll go in the direction that Skinny and the others went."

Drake nodded, but he didn't want to go that way.

The first place they reached was the Hamilton property. The fence on one side of the gate had been cut.

"Nobody was home on Sunday." Drake explained about the horses breaking out of the pasture and said he had checked the house.

"Let's check it again." Pastor Wayne headed toward the porch.

The front door had been pried open, leaving bits of the wood frame littered across the entryway.

"I didn't do this." Drake shook his head.

"I didn't think you had." The pastor entered with his rifle ready.

The living room looked undisturbed, but all the kitchen cabinets and drawers stood open. Several pots, pans, and some broken glass littered the floor. No food remained in the house.

"Mr. Hamilton used to hunt with Dad, but I'll bet we don't find any weapons."

Pastor Wayne nodded.

They did a quick search. The medicine cabinets in the master bedroom stood open, and the contents littered the sink and floor.

"What are you looking for?"

Pastor Wayne didn't answer but continued to check rooms. Several minutes later, he said, "There's no one here. Let's move on."

The next home, a farmhouse set back off the road behind some trees, couldn't be seen from the road.

Together they walked the rutted, dirt driveway. When they rounded a bend, rows of corn, beans, cucumbers, and pumpkins spread out on both sides.

Drake stopped. Behind a pickup truck, a gray-haired man raised a rifle to his shoulder.

"Hey, Michael, Pastor Wayne here." He waved. "Put the gun down."

Michael lowered the weapon and plopped a ball cap on his head. He stepped into the clearing. "My eyes must be getting bad, Preacher. Good to see you." He turned his head. "Annie, Pastor Wayne is here."

"Your eyes aren't bad." Pastor Wayne smiled. "You're just getting ornery in your old age."

Michael laughed. "Maybe so."

With tanned and wrinkled skin, the man seemed to have worked outside all his life. A gray-haired woman hurried from the house. She might have been as old as the man, but her skin had fewer wrinkles.

Pastor Wayne introduced Drake to the couple and then asked if they had seen any prowlers around their place.

"Sure have." Michael shook his head. "Had to shoot at a couple of them."

"We're going to have a meeting at the church this evening at five. I want to set up some sort of neighborhood watch."

"Great idea, Preacher. I'll be there." Michael grinned. "That'll give Annie a chance to shoot the prowlers."

After contacting several other families, Drake and Pastor Wayne came to a mailbox with a honey bee painted on the side.

Together they walked along a narrow, dirt driveway lined with six beehives, three on each side of the lane.

Drake froze at the sight of dozens of bees weaving back and forth over the lane.

"Max uses them as insect guard dogs. I've learned they won't bother you if you don't bother them,"

Drake stayed close to the pastor as he strolled through the buzzing haze.

As they neared the front door a couple in their thirties stepped out.

"Hello, Pastor." The man stepped forward and shook his hand.

"Hello, Emily, Max. How are your bees doing?" Pastor Wayne gestured toward the hives. "This isn't all of your bees, is it?"

Max reached out and the two shook hands. "No, I've got more hives in the back. What brings you here today?"

Four kids, ranging from a boy about five years younger than Drake to a toddler, crowded near the doorway, trying to watch and listen.

Drake had seen them, even talked with the oldest, but didn't really know them.

"Have you seen any prowlers or looters around your place?" Pastor Wayne asked.

"We've seen them." Max nodded.

"Yes!" Emily snarled. "One of them, a really large creep, tried to lure Deb." She pointed to a girl about ten years old.

"I think they're picking soft targets to loot now, but food is getting harder to find." Max frowned. "If things don't change, they may...I hate to think what might happen. God help us all."

"I agree, and God will help us, but while He is doing His part, I've called a meeting for this evening." Pastor Wayne explained about the gathering and Max promised to attend.

After visiting a dozen fairly typical families, all short of food or out, concerned about prowlers, and hoping things would return to normal, Drake and Pastor Wayne arrived at a rusty, faded blue and dirty white mobile home a few feet off the road. Duct tape held a board over part of one dusty window.

"Does anyone live here?" Drake asked.

Pastor Wayne shrugged and then knocked.

The door flew open.

Drake stumbled back.

A man, about thirty years old with messy black hair, stood in the doorway. Arms, dotted with bloody red sores, extended from a threadbare and dirty shirt. "Who are you?" His eyes flared wide.

"I'm Pastor Wayne and—"

"Why are you here? To steal?" As he talked, he scratched his arms and face. "Is that why you have a gun? This is my place, my stuff!"

Drake grasped the sling of his rifle as his heart pounded.

"No." Pastor Wayne shook his head. "That's not why—"

"Are you with the police?"

"No."

What's wrong with this guy? Drake didn't know whether to pull the rifle from his shoulder or grab the pastor and run.

A woman appeared in the doorway, her eyes red and tired; the entirety of her body seemed to sag. "Go back inside, Gordon." She sighed. "I'll talk to them."

She might have been the same age as the man. It was hard to tell. From somewhere in the dark mobile home, a baby cried.

The crazy-eyed man retreated within. "They better not steal nothing."

"I'm sorry about Gordon." She looked over her shoulder. "My name's Gail. He hasn't been well the last couple of days."

Pastor Wayne nodded and explained about the meeting.

"I'll try to be there," the woman mumbled. "But Gordon can't care for the baby right now."

"Bring the infant." Pastor Wayne smiled. "It might be good for both of you to get out of the house for a few hours."

After the woman nodded, Pastor Wayne and Drake left. As they walked, Drake thought about what they had just witnessed. "Was it drugs that caused Gordon to be so weird?"

"Withdrawing from them would be my guess. His supply probably dried up four days ago." Pastor Wayne rested a hand on Drake's shoulder. "That's one reason I suggested she come to the meeting. It'll be best if we get her and the baby away from Gordon. God help them both if they stay with him."

As they neared the far end of Fremont Hill, the paved county road ended and they continued along a paved driveway.

"I've been down this road before." Drake pointed to lines of trees ahead. "The guy, I don't know his name, sells Christmas trees."

Pastor Wayne nodded. "Ben Huntington and his wife, Louise. Years ago he managed a sawmill in Riverbank. He's retired now but still sells trees and has a small mill on his property."

In the clearing, a six-foot, wrought-iron fence surrounded the white, two-story home. Four snarling and barking dogs of different breeds greeted them at the gate.

A trim gray-haired man in jeans and collared shirt stepped out the front door.

"That's Christmas tree guy."

"Good to see you, Ben." Pastor Wayne waved. "Can we talk?"

Ben called the dogs into the house and walked to the gate. "Hi there, Pastor. It's nice to see you."

Ben opened the gate and shook hands with both of them.

"How's the mill?" Pastor Wayne gestured to a large, garage-like building near the house.

"It took me a few days to get the equipment running after the sun storm, but I'm back in business—well, if there is any business. Gas for my generator is the problem now. I'm running low, so I shut the mill down." He shrugged. "Do you think things will get back to normal?"

"Not anytime soon." Pastor Wayne explained about the meeting and invited him and Louise.

"One of us will be there, but someone needs to stay and keep watch over the place. We've had problems with prowlers."

"Everyone has," Drake added.

After visiting a few more homes, they reached a corner and Pastor Wayne gestured to his left. "That way will take us back toward my house."

Drake pointed to Ashley's home up the road. "I'd like to stop there."

The front door of her home had been pried open, just as they had seen at the Hamilton place. Every cabinet door and drawer remained open with seemingly random pots, pans, and cups scattered on the kitchen floor. No food of any sort remained, but that wasn't why Drake had entered. Grasping several cloth shopping bags, he hurried upstairs.

Pastor Wayne followed at a slower pace.

Drake gathered family pictures from around the house, ending in Ashley's room. Then he grabbed more of her clothes from the closet, a few books, and everything left on the top of her dresser and nightstand.

He still had an empty bag.

Drake opened a dresser drawer revealing bras and panties. He felt his face go from warm to burning as he scooped everything out and dropped it into the bag, which then fell over spilling pink and pastel girl clothes on the floor.

He dropped to his knees and hurried to return everything to the bag before Pastor Wayne came looking for him. Then he stuffed a hoodie on top and dashed from the room.

He found Pastor Wayne at the door of the bath. Combs, razors, and creams lay strewn on the floor.

"Was someone looking for drugs?" Drake asked.

"Probably." Pastor Wayne frowned. "Let's head back home."

"Forty-two." Drake smiled at the pastor. "That's how many homes we visited. I counted."

"That's a lot of walking. My feet are tired."

Drake relaxed a bit as they walked up the street. Most of the homes they visited were occupied and most of the people were pleasant. Yes, they were hungry and worried, but almost all of them still tried to be friendly.

Despite all that had happened in the last few days, Drake felt hopeful. He had friends and neighbors and they were planning for better times ahead. Perhaps they could get organized and solve the food and water problems.

As they walked from Ashley's home, a rifle shot crackled through the air.

A woman screamed.

* * *

Portland, Oregon, Thursday, September 8th

Crouching in a shaded doorway across the road, Neal studied the four men who guarded the gate. Three held M4 rifles; one knelt by an M2 machine gun. Their uniforms appeared to be in proper order. He relaxed a bit. They might really be military.

As he continued to watch, a black sedan drove up and the nearest man rendered a proper salute while another opened the gate.

Convinced that they were real soldiers and not some militia group, Neal stood and stepped into the light. "Come on, Ginger." His real map hadn't shown a base in this area, and the hand-sketched one Major Franklin provided didn't indicate the army camp extended this far, but so many things had changed in the last few days.

The dog trotted alongside as he approached the gate with his shotgun over a shoulder and hands in view.

When Neal reached the middle of the street, a sergeant stepped to the gate. "Halt."

The other soldiers all pointed their weapons at him. "My name is Neal Evans. I met Major Franklin south of here in Lebanon. I have a message for his commanding officer." Neal pointed to the letter extending above his shirt pocket. *I should have had it in my hand.* Neal slowly retrieved it and held it up.

The sergeant stepped forward.

Neal snapped his hand back. "I was told by the major to deliver it to his commanding officer, not you." Although certain the sergeant would deliver the letter, Neal hoped to talk to the officer and perhaps get a ride home.

The sergeant frowned but nodded and retreated to an antique field telephone. Neal couldn't hear the words, but the soldier soon returned to the gate.

"Approach with your hands where I can see them."

Neal continued across the street.

"Remove your shotgun and any other weapons." The sergeant stepped closer. "I'll need to inspect your backpack."

Ginger growled.

"Calm down, girl," Neal said in soft tones. "It's okay."

"Will the dog bite?"

Neal shrugged. "She hasn't bitten me."

The sergeant kept his distance. "Hand me your backpack and weapon. You'll get your gun back when you leave."

Moments later, Neal and Ginger sat in the back seat of a jeep, zipping across the compound. It felt strange to hear the rumble of the engine around him and feel the wind on his face. The jeep turned down a gray, industrial street and stopped at a four-story office building nestled tight between two old brick-and-mortar warehouses.

A soldier stepped from the office building, "Neal Evans? I'm Lieutenant Pool. I'll take you to General Sattler."

"Stay." Neal left Ginger with the driver and then followed the lieutenant into the building.

As they stepped inside, the lieutenant spoke again, "We started holding an orientation briefing for new soldiers, marines, and their families who straggle in every day. The general is in the conference room, speaking with them right now. I'll introduce you when he's done."

As they walked down the hall the realization hit Neal. "Lights. You have lights."

Pool smiled. "Yes, the electric grid is down hard, but we have several large generators on the post."

They entered a gleaming white conference room. At the opposite end, a gray-haired man in an army combat uniform stood on a podium. Neal spotted the single star on the chest insignia that identified him as the general. As if in pews of a church, about twenty-five people sat in rows along both sides of the room. Pool pointed to chairs in the back and they both sat. Neal turned his attention to the general pacing back and forth.

"We don't have the manpower to maintain control of the city so we've secured the area around the University of Portland, part of the port, and a large residential area. There are two other, smaller posts near here."

"So, later on, do you plan to expand this area?" a woman asked.

"We hope to restore order to all of Oregon, but food, fuel, and manpower will determine what we do in the near future."

"It's been five days," someone in the group stated.

The general frowned. "A lot has changed in five days."

Neal nodded.

"Some panic-buying began on Saturday with the first announcement about the coming coronal mass ejection." The general sighed and stood in silence for a moment. "Sunday, after the first CME hit, the electric grid went down and we lost most communication. That's also when everyone realized they needed more food, candles, matches, and much more. However, with the power down, stores took only cash. By Sunday night, widespread looting broke out. Police and our soldiers tried to contain it." He shook his head. "Looting continued until there wasn't a grocery store in Portland that had anything left. As I mentioned, we have three positions in the city with plenty of food and MREs for the next few months."

"What about after that?"

"That's exactly the problem. Most people live in cities, but food production is difficult in urban areas. For now, I'm waiting for orders and doing the best I can."

A soldier raised his hand. "General, you mentioned waiting for orders. Do you have communication with command centers?"

"Yes. Relaying messages through Military Auxiliary Radio and civilian ham operators, we have contact with several bases in California and across the country to the Washington, DC, area."

"Do you know if the solar storms are still going on?"

"The University of Portland uses our communication facilities to maintain contact with several other universities and observatories. They all report the same thing. Large solar flares continue on the sun. Several CMEs have hit the earth over the last few days, destroying most modern electronics."

"So this is happening worldwide?" someone asked.

The general nodded. "No one can help us because we're all in the same boat."

Neal felt like he had been punched. While he expected that the solar storms had hit the entire world, the confirmation stunned him. He raised his hand. "Do you have communication with any military or civilians in Western Washington State?"

General Sattler shook his head. "Other than sporadic comms with Lewis-McChord, no." After several more questions, he dismissed the group and turned toward a side door. Lieutenant Pool hurried to the general as Neal followed at a slower pace.

"General, sir, this is Neal Evans. He has a message from Major Franklin."

Neal pulled the envelope from his pocket and handed it over. "I also have a message for Major Franklin's family."

With lips pressed tight and a slow shake of his head, General Sattler read the message. He looked at Neal with a stone face. "Thank you for delivering this. Major Franklin's wife, Carol, and his boys live on this post now. Lieutenant Pool, take our guest to them."

"Yes, sir."

"General, sir, do you have outposts north of here?" Neal asked.

"Yes."

"Could I get a ride with a convoy to your most northern post?"

General Sattler stared at Neal for a moment. "You asked the question about communication with Western Washington state."

"Yes, sir."

"You have family there?"

Neal nodded.

"We owe you that much. Lieutenant Pool, when you two are done at the Franklin home, take him to the Interstate bridge over the Columbia River."

*   *   *

Rural Lewis County, Washington, Thursday, September 8th

A second shot boomed.

Drake dropped the bags just inside the door of Ashley's home and ran several yards toward the shot and scream.

"Stop," Pastor Wayne shouted. Then, in a lower voice, he said, "That wasn't a shotgun and I don't think the voice was anyone from our homes. Get the stuff for Ashley. I don't want to have to come back this way."

Drake retrieved the sacks and together they crept along the road.

An old man across the street hurried back into his house. They hadn't spoken to people up this street and those that saw them looked with fearful eyes as they moved, hunched over, along the fences and among the trees and bushes.

Drake focused his attention to his right in the direction of the blast and scream. Seeing nothing out of the ordinary, he asked, "Didn't it come from over there?" He pointed toward the shot. "Should we move in that direction?"

"I want to check with Mary and Katy and put us between our homes and whoever fired the weapon."

Drake nodded and kept a wary eye to his right as they hurried up the street.

The snarl of a truck engine filled the air.

Drake peered in the direction of the sound. Seconds later, Pastor Wayne's home became visible and a Humvee pulled into his driveway.

Dan, wearing a wide-brimmed hat and long sleeves, stepped from the vehicle. A deputy sheriff exited from the driver's side.

Pastor Wayne hurried to Dan. "Glad you're back safe. Do you know who fired the gun? Who screamed?"

The deputy helped a trembling woman from the Humvee. Her frizzy red hair stood in stark contrast to her ghostly pale skin. Purple, blue, and red bruises blemished her arms and face.

"This is Deputy Campbell," Dan gestured toward the officer. "He fired the gun."

Mary hurried from the house and rushed straight to the red-haired woman. "You look like you need to sit down. Come inside with me." She led her toward the house. "Do you want some water? Maybe tea, if I can get the fire started."

When Drake and the men were alone, Dan said, "I was coming back with Deputy Campbell when we rounded the curve just down the hill." He gestured to the deputy. "Well, I'll let you tell it."

"We encountered a group of four men and a woman, Emily, about to cross the road. When Emily screamed and tried to break free, I stopped and got out. One of them fired at me. She managed to escape from the guy holding her and ran toward me. I fired back at the shooter. The four men then ran into the woods."

"Had they kidnapped her?" Pastor Wayne asked.

The deputy nodded. "South of town yesterday. I don't know much more than that. She's pretty shaken up."

Four kidnappers that close. Drake thought of Ashley as fear and worry rose within him. He wanted to run home and ensure she was safe.

"We're trying to maintain law and order, but it's difficult with no communication." The deputy sighed. "We have enough gas but only a few working vehicles. We had to release twenty-two nonviolent prisoners yesterday."

"You released prisoners?" Drake's heart pounded.

Deputy Campbell nodded. "The jail is running short of food, so the sheriff ordered them released."

Images of his confrontations with Skinny and Fatty mingled in Drake's mind with movies about serial killers and stories of people murdered in their homes.

The deputy shrugged. "I understand you've called a community meeting for Fremont residents. When is it?"

Dan pulled an old-fashioned pocket watch from his jeans. "In about an hour."

"I'll be there," Drake said. "But I've got to get home first." Before anyone could reply, he grabbed the bags for Ashley and sprinted away.

* * *

Lane County, Oregon, Thursday, September 8th

Neal rode with Lieutenant Pool along tree-lined suburban streets where children played. Ginger sat on his lap with her head out the window, sniffing the air. It all seemed so peaceful, so normal. But, in these last few days, such playful innocence had become unusual. "Did Major Franklin live in the area before the solar storm?"

"No. Housing within the compound is in short supply." Pool turned down a side street. "But whenever a home becomes available we move someone in."

"How do homes become available?"

"Well, some people never returned home after the storms; others left for one reason or another; and some have died because of the storms."

"Died? Because of the storm?" Then Neal recalled the dead farmer where he found Ginger. He scratched the dog behind the ears.

"Some people are dying because they can't get medicine or an operation. We expect that will only grow worse over the coming months.

Also, think of the complications that will arise from illnesses such as HIV, diabetes, and even asthma."

Neal shook his head. "A lot more people are going to die."

The lieutenant braked to a stop in front of an older, two-story brown home with a wide porch. Children played kickball in the street nearby.

A woman with streaks of gray in her hair and wearing new jeans opened the door and walked onto the porch.

Lieutenant Pool hopped from the jeep. "Hello, Carol."

"Hi." She smiled, nodded, and then locked eyes on Neal.

"Mrs. Franklin?" Neal climbed from the jeep with Ginger beside him. "I met your husband two days ago. He gave me this for you." He held up the envelope.

Carol's smile grew as she hurried toward him. They met in the front yard and Neal handed her the letter.

"Thank you." Carol tore it open. "Thank you," she repeated as she read.

Two teenage boys stepped onto the porch. They appeared to be about the same age as Neal's sons.

Guilt welled up in Neal. He had gone to the conference mostly to get away from home and had left his sons alone when they needed him the most. At least Conner was there for Drake.

Carol turned to the boys. "Your father is okay. He sends his love." She smiled at Neal. "I'm very grateful you delivered his letter. Can you stay for a while? I don't have much food, but do you need water? I have water and there's a comfortable couch in the living room."

Neal turned to Pool. "It's up to you."

"That'll work out fine. The convoy to the bridge will be leaving later this evening. I'll come back and pick you up."

Carol led Neal toward the house as Lieutenant Pool departed.

"How did you meet Dirk?"

"Well, he arrested me."

She laughed. "You must tell me everything."

They walked through the house to the backyard as Neal told his story. In the yard, they tied Ginger with a long rope to a tree.

"After a soldier looked through my backpack and your husband talked with me … well, I guess he believed me. He wrote notes for General Sattler and for you, and asked me to deliver them."

"I appreciate you doing that for him." She gave Ginger water and then turned. "Follow me and I'll give you water too."

Neal filled his bottles and joined Carol in the living room. He started to make polite conversation, but then leaned back on the couch and sleep soon overtook him.

Long shadows darkened the living room when Neal awoke. He stood and through the window spotted Carol sitting on the porch. He stepped out and sat in a chair nearby.

"Your couch is very comfortable."

"It's not mine. Most of the furniture isn't. The neighbors tell me the couple who lived here were visiting family in Australia." She shook her head. "I can't imagine how they'll get home."

"Well, I'm grateful for the chance to doze on it."

"Where have you been sleeping these last few days?"

"On the ground mostly. I have a tarp and sleeping bag, but it's still sleeping on the ground."

Carol pulled the neatly folded letter from her jean pocket. "Dirk expects the situation to grow much worse before it gets better. You've been out there. Is that what you think?"

Neal's answer came slowly. "Yes." He had encountered so much death and violence. "I think it'll get much worse. Send a letter with the next convoy headed in your husband's direction. He'll be relieved to know you're safe."

She grimaced. "Safe? Is there such a thing now?"

Lieutenant Pool stopped in front of the house. Neal collected Ginger and his backpack, thanked Carol, and departed.

Sandbags piled against a chain-link fence blocked most of his view of a large modern church just outside the main gate. Several hundred men, women, and children filled the parking lot along the tan, brick two-story building. Dozens more milled about in the road. Soldiers worked to clear the way as the trucks ahead honked and inched forward.

Neal gazed right and left. "There were only a few people at the other gate. Why are so many here?"

"The church has been a relief center. They give out food and refer life-threatening medical cases to us. We also act as security around the church, so many refugees stay nearby."

Staring at the homeless humanity, Neal nodded.

The convoy turned onto the main boulevard.

"Also, we sometimes let people in through this gate," Pool added.

"Who?" Neal asked.

"People with skills we need, like plumbers, electricians, carpenters, and others."

Ten men with close-cut hair and multiple tattoos walked across the street in front of the jeep. As Neal watched, they turned toward the gate to the compound.

"Is the base secure?"

Pool shrugged. "As secure as it can be, I guess. Securing the perimeter is a continuous project. We're constructing a fence, using cargo containers, and converting buildings into watchtowers, but it's less than half complete. I don't know if we can finish it before things turn really ugly."

*   *   *

Cle Elum, Washington, Thursday, September 8th

Conner nudged his way into the laundry room of the Catholic church. He stifled a sneeze as the smell of mold, dust, and old clothes assaulted his nostrils.

His gear hung from one arm and he carried a bowl in each hand. Two spoons protruded from his jean pocket. Once inside, he pushed the door shut with a foot and looked for Madison. Shelves cluttered with shoes, pants, shirts, and coats donated by locals for the homeless and refugees blocked much of his view.

"Madison?"

"Over here."

Conner weaved his way toward the sound of splashing and found Madison in the back corner, washing clothes in a deep sink. He held up the bowls. "The last of the stew."

As she dried her arms, he stared at the dripping faucet. "I wonder how long it will flow."

She shrugged. "Father Dan says the town reservoir is higher in the hills. So, for now, the town has water."

Conner passed her a bowl and spoon and then dropped his backpack in the corner. "Speaking of Father Dan, he says we can sleep here again as long as we don't break any of the commandments."

Madison wiped the spoon with her hand. "I wasn't planning on breaking any … well, any of the ones I know." She smiled at him and sat on a nearby counter.

"You can have the sleeping bag. I'll make a bed with some of these coats."

They ate in silence for several minutes. Then Conner held the bowl to his mouth and slurped the last of the stew. "Father Dan thinks it's safer here and we should stay."

"Would you stay here just because it's safe?" Madison spooned out the last of the broth.

"No." Conner unrolled the sleeping bag. "I left my little brother alone. I've got to get back to him." He pointed to the shelves. "Toss me a few coats and I'll make my bed."

"My parents are older. They're going to need my help." Madison set both bowls on the counter. "I need to get home to Olympia." She grinned and tossed a coat at his head.

Conner caught it with one hand. "Okay, then. Tomorrow at first light we head toward the pass."

After throwing several more coats at him, Madison slid into the sleeping bag.

Conner lay down a couple of feet from her, closed his eyes, and smiled. It felt good to have her close again.

* * *

Rural Lewis County, Washington, Thursday, September 8th

As Drake ran home, he reached into his pocket for the key. Again he had forgotten it. When he neared the house, he took deep breaths and knocked on the door like he would a neighbor's.

Hearing Ashley hurry toward the door, Drake waved at the peephole.

She greeted him with the shotgun in hand but at least not pointed at him.

Once inside, Drake leaned his rifle in the corner and put the bags beside it. Then he sat on the couch and gestured for Ashley to sit beside him. As the next few minutes passed, Drake talked about all the different and unusual neighbors he had met while walking with Pastor Wayne.

When he finished, she asked, "What's in those bags you brought?"

He grinned, reached over the edge of the couch, and grabbed them. "Stuff from your house that I thought you might like."

She pulled out toiletries from her bathroom and then a framed picture of her parents. Tears rolled down her cheeks.

"I'm sorry. I thought it would make you happy."

"It did, silly." She leaned close and kissed him on the cheek. "Thank you."

"I could get more things."

* * *

Less than an hour later, Drake sat at the back of the old church, counting. *Fifty-five.* Pastor Wayne wanted to know how many people attended the meeting and counting distracted him from thoughts of Ashley. *Fifty-six.* He wished there had been more time before the meeting.

Two more walked in followed by Pastor Wayne.

"Fifty-eight people are here so far, including Gail and the baby from the trailer with the weird druggie."

Pastor Wayne wrote notes on a pad as they both walked toward the front of the church. "I'm glad Gail's here. How's Ashley?"

"Ashley?" Just minutes earlier they had been talking and laughing. Then the church bell had rung and he had left her behind once again. "She's fine. I wish we didn't have to guard the property—that it was safer."

"That is what this meeting is about." Pastor Wayne grinned, scribbled more in his notebook.

Deputy Campbell approached the pastor and whispered. "A lot of people are asking me about food, water, and electricity."

Pastor Wayne nodded. "I'd like to know about those too."

"I don't have contact with the outside world, so I don't have those answers. The utility workers I've spoken with tell me we produce only a fraction of our power locally and nothing is coming in from out of the area. They expect the power grid to be down for at least a few months."

"And the food situation?" Pastor Wayne asked.

"Nothing is coming in and every day more people run out of food."

"Does anyone have a plan?" Pastor Wayne rubbed his chin. "The city council, sheriff, or the military?"

The deputy shrugged.

This guy is Deputy Downer. Drake stepped closer as he listened to the somber words.

"Beyond that, the jail is running low on food. We've started releasing low-risk offenders and gang activity is increasing."

This repeated news Drake already new, but it still hit him like a punch in the gut.

The pastor shook his head. "Don't tell these people that. They have enough to worry about." His gaze fell upon Drake. "And not a word of this from you, young man." The pastor returned his gaze to the deputy. "Don't lie, but put your best spin on the news. If you need help, I'll jump in. Go ahead and sit down. I'll start the meeting."

Drake sat in the nearly empty front pew next to the deputy.

"Welcome, everyone." Pastor Wayne smiled. "I'm glad to see so many of you here tonight. My son, Dan, invited Lewis County Deputy Campbell here to provide information about the current situation and how we can help each other here on Fremont Hill."

Pastor Wayne moved to one side as Deputy Campbell stepped to the center of the podium.

Someone in the pews shouted, "When will the power come back on?" Others asked questions in rapid, overlapping succession.

Deputy Campbell held up his hand. "We're working to establish communication with Olympia, but right now I can't give you a definite answer about the power."

"I'm out of food," a woman shouted. "What can I do? What's going to happen?"

Deputy Campbell stared at the crowd. Drake knew the answers to her questions. Little food was available and there would be less with each passing day. She might starve.

Pastor Wayne moved to the center. "There's still food, but we need to cooperate, share and be generous. Save seeds. Plant a garden. If you have a greenhouse, use it." He paused and gazed at the now silent crowd. "We can get through this if we work together."

"How can the government just leave us like this?" a man asked.

"Sit down, Chuck," someone yelled. "It's not the government's job to feed you."

"They're supposed to take care of us." Chuck shook his head but sat. "That's why we pay taxes."

Several people groaned.

"What about the criminals we're seeing?" another asked.

"Difficult times bring out bad people." The deputy shrugged. "That's always been true, but most of your local law enforcement remains on duty. We have several police cars and the Humvee running but, without electricity, the phones, computers, and radios are down."

"What should we do?" someone asked.

"I recommend you establish a community watch program," Deputy Campbell answered.

"I think that's a good start." Pastor Wayne nodded.

"This just won't do!" Chuck shot to his feet again.

"Shut up," another man shouted. "I want to hear what the deputy has to say before it gets too dark to see him."

Drake glanced out a window. The sun stood just above the nearby trees. He estimated they had a few hours of daylight remaining.

"The government is supposed to protect us," Chuck grumbled as he sat.

The meeting progressed, but Chuck stormed out before it ended. Everyone else stayed until the sun stood just above the horizon. Drake felt they left thinking the situation was dire but feeling hopeful.

Drake dashed home as the shadows of twilight deepened. He wished he had never heard Deputy Downer's whispered comments to Pastor Wayne.

Day six

Portland, Oregon, late Thursday into Friday, September 9th

Neal had visited Portland on more occasions than he could recall, but he knew this trip across the city would remain fixed in his mind forever.

The sun fell below most of the building before the before the convoy departed. The streets of Portland became dark manmade canyons.

Neal tensed as the vehicles raced into the darkness.

Occasionally, they would pass a group huddled around a fire. Other times people stood in the road, waving for the trucks to stop, but the convoy never did. The vehicles wove around abandoned cars and surprised pedestrians, often with Ginger barking or growling from the back seat. If something blocked the way, the lead truck, equipped with a plow, pushed it aside.

"Why don't you clear the roads and make this trip faster?" Neal asked.

"We are." Lieutenant Pool steered down a side street following the convoy. "But we change routes frequently."

Stars dotted the sky as the convoy rolled onto the freeway. Pool glanced up. "I've lived in Portland for five years and never seen so many stars."

Neal gazed into the darkness and pointed. "That's Orion, the Big Dipper is there, and if you follow those two stars out you find the North Star."

Pool raised an eyebrow. "Is astronomy a hobby or a profession?"

"A hobby. I've lived in the country most of my life and been a backyard astronomer since I was a boy." However, as Neal continued to stare into the night, his only thought was thankfulness that no aurora weaved across the sky. Tonight no sun storms would inflict additional damage upon mankind.

In the early hours of Friday morning, the convoy left the freeway and proceeded along side streets to an area of hotels beside the Columbia River. The trucks continued down the road, but Lieutenant Pool steered the jeep into a parking lot and stopped. Before either man stepped out, soldiers poured from the nearest hotel and flowed around the jeep, like water around a boulder in a stream. "What's going on?" Pool called to another lieutenant.

"Gunfire across the river in Washington state. We're securing the bridge."

Lieutenant Pool exited the jeep and waved for Neal to follow. Together they climbed to an observation post beside the bridge. There, Pool borrowed binoculars from one of the sentries.

The lieutenant leaned against a chest-high wall of sandbags and stared across the dark water.

Neal followed and stood beside him. "What do you see?"

"Muzzle flashes and small fires." He set the binoculars on the sandbags and looked at Neal with worried eyes. "No one will be crossing this bridge for a while."

Neal leaned onto his elbows. His home state was within sight, but he couldn't get there. He thought of Conner and Drake, alone and afraid.

His wife, Beth, had been the hub around which the family revolved. When she died, they had bumped along, but only just. He had been there for his sons physically but not emotionally.

He had failed them when they needed him the most.

He had failed to protect Beth from the mugger and he had failed the boys.

He was a failure as a man.

* * *

Cle Elum, Washington, Friday, September 9th

Conner yawned and pulled open the back door to the church. The cool of night still embraced the air that flowed in through the door.

Madison stepped out but paused on the porch. "Should we say goodbye before we go?"

"I didn't see anyone awake." Conner looked back for a moment and then let go of the door.

"Wait," a voice called from inside. The door clicked shut and then immediately opened. Father Dan breathed deeply as he stepped out. "I've got good news." He waved Conner and Madison back in.

"A local rancher, Jason, somehow got his truck running and is headed to the west side of the mountains to bring his daughter and son-in-law home. He says you can ride in the back of the truck if you like."

Conner looked at Madison as she nodded and grinned. "Yes," he said to Father Dan. "That would be a great help."

"Good. Wait in the parking lot. I'll go make the final arrangements." He hurried away.

Conner and Madison walked to the empty gravel parking lot. Standing near the middle, Conner pulled off the backpack and set it on the ground. "Well, I'm glad I won't be carrying that on my back all day."

Madison nodded and kicked at a stone. With her head still down, she spoke. "When you find your family, maybe you could come back to Olympia sometime. I'd like to know you arrived home and that your family was okay."

Her words made Conner happy. "Sure, that would be great." He grinned, but more than anything he needed to get home. With each passing day, he felt growing guilt over leaving Drake. Pulled between feelings for Madison and duty to Drake, Conner's gut twisted in a knot.

Father Dan returned with a green backpack and a sleeping bag tied on top. He handed both to Madison. "There's a coat, blanket, and socks in the pack. I thought you'd need it. Jason will be here in a moment."

"Thank you." Madison hugged Father Dan. "It'll be a big help."

Conner heard the sound of an auto engine in the distance.

Father Dan clutched each of their hands and said a prayer. Then he embraced Madison and shook Conner's hand.

An older red pickup stopped beside the three of them. A man with several days of black and gray stubble stepped out from the driver's side.

A teen with only the barest hint of a beard exited from the passenger seat holding a shotgun.

Conner grinned inwardly. The boy really was riding shotgun.

"Hi. I'm Jason." The older man thrust out his hand and shook Conner's. "This is my son, Tim. Father Dan says you need a ride over the mountains. Seems most people are trying to get out of the Seattle area." He shrugged. "But I can give you a ride if you want."

"We do." Conner picked up his backpack. "We both have family over there."

"Family … times like this there's nothing more important." Jason slapped the side of his pickup. "That's why I worked so hard to get the truck running again. I've got family over there too. Well, jump in the back."

Conner and Madison thanked Jason and Madison hopped in the back. Conner grabbed both backpacks and handed them to Madison and then he climbed aboard. With their backs against the cab, they faced the way they had come. Madison rested her head on Conner's shoulder. He wrapped his arm around her as the pickup thumped across potholes and over bumps through town. Within minutes, they sped up an onramp, onto the deserted freeway and higher into the Cascade Mountains.

With the wind blowing around him, Conner whispered. *God, is Dad home? If he isn't, please get him safely there real soon and please keep Drake safe. I'm coming home.*

* * *

Rural Lewis County, Washington, Friday, September 9th

Drake woke up to a tongue rolling across his face, followed by a snort of dog breath.

"Gruff, come," Ashley commanded from some distant room.

He heard the dog trot from the bedroom as he opened his eyes and wiped his wet face. *I've got to make sure to shut my bedroom door at night.*

The house had been dark and quiet when he returned home. Thankful that he had remembered the keys, he had opened the door to Gruff wagging his tail. Ashley lay asleep on the couch. Her shotgun leaned against the nearby wall.

He draped a blanket over her and climbed into his bed.

Hours later, Gruff awoke him with a lick across the face. He felt tired as he rolled out of bed, dressed, and went to find Ashley.

He found her mixing flour and baking powder at the kitchen counter. Gruff curled up on the wood floor beside her, his tail thumping.

She looked up and smiled. "I didn't hear you come in last night and checked your room. Did you finally remember to bring your keys?"

"Yeah, we need a knock or signal." He sat on a stool beside her. "I don't want you to shoot me some night when I come home."

Ashley mixed eggs and goat's milk into the bowl. "Tell me what happened at the meeting."

Drake did but tried to put a less depressing spin on the news.

She shook her head. "Food is running out. Gangs are trying to control Riverbank. The police and sheriff are struggling to keep control. Is that what you're saying?"

"Well, yeah, but—"

"Just give it to me straight. I need to know."

Her words were strong, but her face looked grim.

"Okay." Still, Drake tried to think of some good news. "We formed a neighborhood watch. Four people are going to always be on patrol until things get better. I volunteered to be one of them."

"That's good." Ashley's grin faded quickly. "But how long do we have to do things like that? When will things get better?"

"Ah, the deputy said it might be months … or longer."

Her face lost color as she nodded and then stared out the kitchen window in silence.

"It may take months, but things will get better." Drake's attempt at comfort hung in the air as mere words.

Ashley wiped her eyes. "I've been thinking these last few days … my parents … they aren't coming home, are they?"

Drake squeezed her hand. Maybe they were both orphans, alone in a broken world.

* * *

Portland, Oregon, Saturday, September 9th

Neal awoke to Ginger growling. Rubbing his eyes, he recalled that he'd gone to find a tree near the observation post to wait for the bridge to open. He blinked at the morning sunlight. Ginger stood at the end of her rope, snarling at a sentry.

"The bridge is open. Refugees from the Washington state side say a gang war broke out last night. There seems to be a ceasefire right now, but are you sure you want to walk into that?"

"Yeah, I'm sure." Neal grimaced as he stood. Walking into a battle reminded him of the park near the Lebanon Walmart. Images of dead flashed through his mind. Still, he had to go. His boys needed him. Neal gathered his gear. With Ginger trotting at his side, they jogged to the bridge.

A steady flow of people plodded from the chaos and violence of Vancouver across the bridge into the relative peace of Portland. The sentries inspected those heading south, into Portland, and all but ignored Neal and the few others heading north into Washington state.

When he reached the far side, Neal stopped and drew in a deep breath of Washington air. He estimated that maybe two days of hiking remained ahead of him, but he could almost feel the end of the journey. He would soon be home with his sons. A weight of worry lifted from him. However, before he left Vancouver, he would have a quick visit with his old navy buddy, Josh.

Neal walked several miles along a highway clear of vehicles. A few dozen men, women, and children, some in family groups, hiked along the pavement as if it were a wide sidewalk. Everyone avoided Neal, and occasional growls from Ginger reinforced his isolation. Neal liked that fine because he wanted to move fast.

In the rural areas, Neal expected quiet but, with only the rustle of the breeze in his ears as he walked along the urban highway, the silence felt unnatural, even foreboding. The dark office buildings that lined the freeway only added to the uneasiness within him.

A drizzle of rain tapped his face. Remembering the fires that burned Eugene, he thanked God he didn't have to run ahead of flames.

After a few miles of hiking along the freeway, Neal spotted the exit to Josh's home and hastened down the off ramp to the side streets. At the first intersection, he looked right and then left. Probably because he had always driven here, and from a different direction, distances and directions seemed longer and unfamiliar. He started down one street but decided it didn't look right and walked the other way. Doors hung ajar, and windows were broken on many of the homes. As he passed, armed guards watched from several streets.

The drizzle increased to a light rain. Dark clouds billowed above. Neal hurried in the hope of finding Josh and a safe haven from the rain.

Minutes later, he turned left onto Josh's street. The doors of several houses swayed back and forth in the breeze; others hung by a single hinge. Bullet holes punctured windows and walls. Some homes might have been looted, but others appeared untouched.

Plywood covered the living room window of Josh's single-story red home. Everything else appeared normal. Had Josh put it there? Had his window been shot and broken?

"Come on, Ginger, let's investigate." The rain increased as Neal crossed the lawn to the front of the home. His first knock on the door caused it to creak open. "Josh? Are you okay?" he mumbled and stepped into the dark house. As his eyes adjusted to the dimness, he turned toward the living room.

Floorboards squeaked.

"Is that you, Josh? It's me—"

Something slammed into the back of his head.

Stars danced across his vision.

His knees buckled.

Neal collapsed.

* * *

West of Cle Elum, Washington, Friday, September 9th

The air grew cool as the truck rumbled toward the pass. Refugees, most on foot, some on bikes and a few in cars and trucks, dotted the freeway. Conner pointed as an ancient school bus, packed with people and belongings, rolled east toward Cle Elum.

The temperature continued to fall and soon Conner spotted Keechelus Lake. They would soon reach the summit. He looked for a sign or something that announced the pass, but sitting in the bed of the truck, he saw only the back of road signs. However, buildings and a clear slope marked the ski resort. Soon afterward, he could tell the truck had gone over the pass and now rolled down the western slope.

Due to the rush of the wind, Conner moved close and spoke in Madison's ear. "We're over the summit."

She nodded and smiled.

Conner did some quick figuring in his head. Depending upon how far they traveled by truck, he could be home in two days or less. He smiled. They might reach Madison's home in just over a day. He stared at her face, trying to fix every bit of it in his memory.

She turned and smiled at him.

His face warmed.

She kissed him on the cheek.

Conner hugged her tight. "We need to stay warm." He grinned. If this would be his last full day with her, he'd try to enjoy it.

After traveling several more miles Jason pulled the truck off at a wide spot in the road.

Grateful for the chance to stretch, Conner stood.

"Why are we stopping?" Madison asked.

Jason held up a thermos and cup. "Too much coffee." He disappeared into nearby woods, while his son Tim stood next to the pickup with his shotgun.

Conner jumped out and lowered the tailgate. Madison climbed down.

Spotting the marking for an observation point on a nearby knoll, Conner grabbed his rifle and hiked up a short trail. Madison joined him and together they gazed south along the Cascade Mountains toward home. Towering gray clouds rolled up from the south.

A cold wind blew.

Madison leaned close.

Conner hugged her tight.

"Stop," Tim shouted. A shotgun blast boomed.

Conner yanked the rifle from his shoulder.

Five men, covered with tattoos on their arms and faces, formed a semi-circle along the road and edged near Tim and the truck. No one seemed hurt. Had Tim fired into the air?

Jason darted from the woods, holding a pistol.

Leading with his rifle, Conner hurried across the gravel, keeping the truck between him and the men.

"We were just admiring your pickup." One of the tattooed men stepped forward and pulled a pistol from his pocket.

"Admire it from a distance." Jason hopped in the driver's seat and started the truck. "Tim, get in the cab."

Another man pulled a pistol.

Conner jumped into the bed of the pickup and Madison followed.

Gravel sprayed as Jason accelerated back toward the pavement.

Conner stumbled to his knees and then yanked up the tailgate.

A thud shook the pickup.

Pistol fire mixed with a shotgun blast.

As they raced away, Conner glimpsed one of the gang members on the ground.

Another gang member fired a shot.

Conner returned fire and fell backward in the bed of the truck.

As the pickup sped down the road, Conner moved in front of Madison. With his rifle over the tailgate, he tried to return fire, but the bounce and sway of the truck defeated his attempt to aim.

For nearly an hour, Jason traveled along paved roads and stopped for nothing. Then he reduced his speed as he turned onto a gravel lane, and slowed even more as he turned up a driveway. When he pulled alongside a white, two-story farmhouse, he eased to a stop. Jason stepped from the cab. "This is my daughter and son-in-law's place."

Conner clutched his rifle. *Why hasn't anyone come out to greet us?*

Jason walked to the front door and knocked. "Sue … Raymond … are you there?"

He banged harder on the door.

No one answered.

* * *

Rural Lewis County, Washington, Friday, September 9th

Within seconds, tears flowed down Ashley's cheeks. "I was mad at Mom and Dad on Saturday." She sniffled. "I don't know why, but I always seemed to be angry with them lately." She wiped her eyes with a hand.

Unsure of what to say, Drake passed her a box of tissues.

Ashley dabbed her eyes. "They told me to stay home Saturday night. I wanted to do what I wanted—go to your party." She sighed and wiped her eyes again. "I wanted them to leave ... just disappear ... and they did."

Watching her, Drake nearly cried. With each passing day, it became less likely his father and brother would ever return. Fighting back his own tears, he held Ashley until her sobs ceased.

Even with Ashley nestled against him, Drake felt empty and abandoned, but he would hold back his tears for Ashley's sake.

Later, alone in the barn, Drake allowed himself to mourn for his missing father and brother and even his long-dead mother. Without them, he felt small in a really big and scary world. He banged on the wood shelf with his fist, spilling feed and grain. Tears rolled down his cheeks and dripped onto the bench.

No. He shook his head and wiped his eyes. He must be strong for Ashley. When the tears had faded to sniffles, he finished his chores and, with a final wipe of a sleeve across his face, walked toward the house. They might be alone in the world, but he would do his best for Ashley.

Few words passed between the two as the day slid by. Ashley worked on training Gruff in the morning and then again in the afternoon and prepared meals. Drake read his father's notebooks, cared for the livestock, and checked survival gear, food stocks, and weapons.

I haven't ever studied this hard. He slid the notebook aside, stood, and grabbed his rifle. Intending to do afternoon chores, he walked toward the back.

A knock sounded from the front door.

Ashley hurried into the living room with her shotgun.

Gruff growled.

Fairly certain that bad guys wouldn't knock, Drake crept toward the entry and peered out the peephole. "It's Pastor Wayne." He opened the door and invited him in.

"Can you go on a short hike with me?" Pastor Wayne pointed toward the highest point on Fremont Hill. "I've got something I want to show you."

Drake looked at Ashley. He always seemed to be leaving her.

"It won't take long," Pastor Wayne added.

Ashley smiled. "I'll see you in a little bit."

Drake followed Pastor Wayne along a trail through the forest. The path emerged near a new wire-mesh fence secured to thick, wood posts that ran along the ridgeline. He imagined it would be hard to climb the slope to the fence, but the height of the mesh, well over Drake's head, and rolled barbed wire along the top would make entry through here very difficult. They followed the fence and soon arrived at the remnants of a stone wall built into a rock outcrop at the southwest corner of the hill.

"I've been here before." Drake hurried ahead. "When I was a kid, I'd play here with friends. This is Fort Fremont, isn't it?"

"What's left of it. They demolished most of it after World War I. The commander's house is over there." Pastor Wayne pointed to a small stone building with no roof or doors.

Drake walked among the ruins and then to the boulders that looked over Riverbank, several miles of freeway, and the Chehalis River that flowed along the south of the town.

"Where did you get all this fence stuff?"

"Remember Ben Huntington, the Christmas tree guy? He milled the posts and is doing more. Another man at the meeting, Rob Gunther, manages a farm supply warehouse in town. He had the fence."

"Did you guys do all this work? Are you trying to fence in the hill?"

"A dozen people worked on it, including me." Pastor Wayne grinned. "Yes, we're trying to protect the Fremont Hill community. We did a lot today, but there's much more to do. By tomorrow evening we plan to have a simple plywood roof over this observation post and we'll be extending the fences north and east from here."

"I can help."

"I planned to ask you." Pastor Wayne rested one hand on Drake's shoulder and pointed with the other. "That stretch of the fence will run east and eventually go along the back of your property."

"My property?" A week ago, Drake was a kid playing video games, and the farm belonged to his father. Sadness surged within him. Was it really his farm now?

Pastor Wayne pointed along the fence line. "Is it okay if we continue?"

"Yes, but I want to be there when you build it."

"Of course." Pastor Wayne turned and gazed at the town and river below.

Drake leaned on the boulder and gazed at Riverbank and the freeway. His father had once said that the difference between a man and a boy was accepting responsibility. If he had inherited the farm, and the responsibilities of a man, it all felt overwhelming.

Moments later, the sunlight faded like a dimmer switch being turned down. He looked up as gray storm clouds rolled toward them.

Drake shivered.

* * *

King County, Washington, Friday, September 9th

Conner watched as Jason pulled a key from one pocket and a pistol from the other. He knocked again, but when no one answered, he used the key to enter. Warily, Conner and the others followed and did a quick search of the house.

Minutes later, Jason walked into the dining room. "Did you find anything?"

Conner shook his head. "Nothing suspicious. There's even food in the kitchen."

"Why would Sue and Raymond leave?" Jason asked as Tim and Madison walked into the room.

"We should search the barn and greenhouse," Tim said.

Madison stood beside Conner. "We'll help you look."

Conner nodded. It seemed to him that criminals would have taken the food and made a mess doing it. "They might be headed to Cle Elum, but sure, we should check outside."

The four left through the back door.

"Sue and Raymond just keep a few acres of pasture for their horses." Jason gazed at the farmyard. "They lease the cornfield to the old couple on the next farm. They might be there."

"They would have seen us heading down the road," Conner said. "But I'll walk toward that farm."

Tim headed to the barn, and Jason strode toward a large greenhouse.

Madison pointed to what appeared to be a toolshed with an Old West-style water pump beside it. "I'll check that out."

Conner ambled along with her in the direction of the shed and past the water pump. He bent low and slid through the barbed wire fence into the cornfield. The crop stood taller than he did, ready for harvest in a few weeks. He strolled along one row and over to another, not expecting to find anything. He stirred up small clouds of dust as he walked.

After a couple of minutes, he could see the next farmhouse but no one outside. While trying to decide how to approach the home, something hard pushed against the back of his head.

"That's the barrel of my shotgun at the base of your skull." The man thumped Conner's back as if to reinforce the point. "Drop the rifle and put your hands up."

Conner did as commanded, but someone grabbed the rifle before it hit the ground.

"Don't turn around or move suddenly," the man instructed. "How many are with you?"

Determined not to tell him anything useful, Conner shook his head. "We don't want any trouble. We're not here to hurt anyone."

"We'll see about that. Go back toward the house you came from—slowly."

It irritated Conner that twice in a week a gun had been pointed at him, but fear moved him to do as told. With his hands up, he turned and walked back. The man had managed to stay out of sight. Only he had spoken, but Conner thought he heard two people moving behind him. His pace slackened.

"Keep going." The gun barrel jabbed into Conner's back.

"Don't hurt him," a woman pleaded.

A man and a woman? Could they be—?

Madison stepped out of the cornstalks twenty feet ahead. Her eyes widened as she turned to run. Conner felt the gun barrel scrape across his back. Near his right shoulder, the end veered into view. In a single flowing motion, Conner spun backward, ducked under the barrel, and knocked it skyward.

It fired with a boom.

For an instant, Conner faced his assailant, a man only a few years older than himself. Before the man could rack the shotgun, Conner kicked his knee and grabbed the firearm.

As the man fell, Conner yanked the weapon free. Stepping back, he shifted his aim to the woman. Her eyes were wide, but she held Conner's rifle in her hands. "Drop the weapon and put your hands up."

She hesitated.

Conner didn't want to hurt anyone, but he didn't want her to shoot him either. He pointed the barrel at her head.

"No!" Sitting on the ground, the man thrust out his palms, pleading. "Don't hurt her, please!"

She dropped the rifle onto the dusty ground.

Conner heard movement behind him and glanced over his shoulder.

"Are you okay?" Madison stepped forward and retrieved the weapon from the ground.

He nodded.

Hearing more movement, Conner looked down the row of corn. Jason and Tim ran toward them.

"Sue … Raymond … I'm so glad they found you," Jason shouted.

Conner stared at Raymond as the horror of what could have happened tore through him, "I could have killed you."

Raymond stood, wobbled, and rubbed his knee. "Who are you two?"

"Friends," Madison said flatly.

Conner handed the shotgun back to Raymond as Jason hugged Sue.

Tim followed close behind.

As they all neared the farmhouse, Sue pointed at the pickup. "Is that your truck, Dad?"

"Sure is." Jason nodded. "One of my old farm trucks. I had to replace the starter and battery, but now it runs well."

"We didn't recognize it." Raymond shook his head. "When we saw it coming up the road, I grabbed the shotgun and we hurried out the back."

"Why?" Tim asked. "You were armed."

"We didn't want to be trapped in the house by some gang," Sue said as they climbed the steps. "Groups have been raiding homes in the area for food and drugs."

Standing on the back porch, Raymond turned to Conner. "I'm sorry I pointed my gun at you." His face flushed.

"You didn't know." Conner didn't feel he had anything to apologize for, but in the spirit of the moment, he decided to return the gesture. "I'm sorry if I hurt your knee and for pointing a gun at you and Sue."

Next, it seemed that everyone was apologizing for both real and perceived wrongs. Laughter ensued as they entered the house.

When the amusement faded, Sue asked, "Why are you here, Dad?"

"To bring you home. It isn't safe this close to Seattle. Better for both of you to be on our place, with family. There's plenty of room."

"I couldn't leave our horses."

"The truck has a hitch. Hook up your trailer, pack up your things, and let's get going."

Raymond nodded agreement.

Sue looked doubtful.

Feeling a tug on his sleeve, Conner turned to Madison.

With her head, she motioned for him to follow and together they went into the living room. "I figured this is a family matter they need to discuss."

"Sure." Conner sat beside her on a couch and, for the next few minutes, they planned their route.

Raymond stepped into the room. "Sue has started packing. We'll be headed back over the mountains soon." He opened a closet and pulled out a box. "Before we go though, I have some camping food and some gear in here that you can have."

"Thanks." Conner took the box.

The sun peaked in the sky and began its downward trek while Jason attached the horse trailer, Sue filled boxes and suitcases and Conner and Madison packed food into their packs and filled canteens at the water pump.

Sue unlocked the toolshed and swung open the door with a loud creak. "I thought you two might need these."

Madison smiled.

Conner looked over his shoulder at Sue holding two expensive-looking red bicycles.

"Yes." Conner nodded.

"We haven't used them in years. Not since we bought the horses." Sue pushed them forward to Conner. "We don't have room for them."

"Thank you." Madison smiled. "It would have been a long walk."

Jason loaded the horses and then squeezed into the back of the pickup with his wife, various suitcases, and a couple of dozen boxes.

Conner and Madison waved goodbye and then turned south on their new bikes toward home.

Day seven

Clark County, Washington, Saturday, September 10th

The darkness faded and Neal returned to consciousness with a pounding headache. His eyes fluttered open to a view of Ginger's belly. He tried to understand both why his head hurt and why Ginger stood across his face, growling.

Something had hit the back of his head.

He pushed the dog aside and sat up. His head throbbed and the world swayed, but he managed to remain upright.

Ginger growled toward a dark corner.

As his eyes adjusted to the dim light, a woman in a loose jacket, holding a shotgun, gradually became visible.

Neal glanced about for his weapon.

"Yeah, this is your shotgun," the woman said. "You dropped it and I grabbed it before that dog of yours came at me."

"Well, you did hit me." The face of the woman showed fear, but with his shotgun across her lap, he didn't want to challenge her too much. Neal casually brushed the side of his jacket. His pistol remained in place. "Who are you?"

"This house belongs to my family." She lifted the shotgun with both hands. *"Who are you?"*

"Your house?" Neal rubbed the back of his head. Could this be the wrong place? He looked about and spotted pictures of Josh and his family. As he did, one photo in particular caught his attention. He looked back and forth between the woman and the picture. "Are you Claire?"

"How do you know my name?"

"Because I'm a friend of your dad. I'm Neal."

She stood revealing a bulging belly. "Neal?" She stepped closer with the gun limp at her side. "Dad said you might be coming but … well, that was a week ago."

Ginger snarled and she moved back. "I've always liked dogs, but this one might change my mind."

"Calm down, Ginger." Neal pulled the dog back toward him. "I've had to walk a lot to get here. Where's Josh?"

"Tie up the dog and follow me."

Claire handed Neal his shotgun and then led him up a dark stairwell to the master bedroom.

Sunlight from a window illuminated the room. Josh's head rested on a pillow. The rest of him lay hidden under several blankets.

"Is he dead?" Neal asked.

"Not yet," Josh mumbled. "Is that you, Neal? I can't see so well."

"Yes, it's me." Neal stepped to the side of the bed. "What happened to you? How can I help?"

No answer came from his friend.

Across from Neal, Claire drew close to the bed. She pulled up a chair, sat, and clutched her father's hand. "He's been drifting in and out of consciousness for a day now."

"Is he dying?" Neal cringed as he asked the question with his friend on the bed before him. "How did he get hurt?"

"He's never managed his diabetes well."

"I knew he was diabetic, but why is it killing him?"

"I'm not sure of all the details. He's a stubborn man and doesn't talk much about his illnesses, especially the diabetes. I'm pretty sure that's what is killing him … but … well, it's more complicated than that." She let out a deep breath and continued. "I came down to visit him from Everett last weekend. When the news of the sun storms broke, Dad encouraged me to stay just in case things got bad." She sighed and shook her head. "Things sure did get bad. A couple of days later, I could tell he wasn't well. I finally got him to admit that he had run out of insulin." She stroked her father's hand."

"I'm sure we can get more."

Josh shuddered, but his eyes remained closed.

"I've checked with the VA hospital. They're doing triage of all patients and are saving the insulin for children and people less dependent on the drug—not old guys with type 1 diabetes and lung cancer."

"Cancer?" The word hit Neal like a blow to the gut. "I didn't know. I haven't visited in years, but we've exchanged phone calls, emails, and Christmas cards."

"I guess that's not the kind of thing he wanted to say in a card, email, or call."

Neal nodded. "I should have visited, but I've been busy … since Beth died." Neal knew that wasn't true. Since she had died, he had struggled to maintain connections with anyone, even his sons.

"Sometimes people drift apart, but I think Dad wanted to reconnect with you on this visit and say goodbye."

After talking with Claire some more, Neal brought water and food to Ginger and returned to the bedroom. He pulled up a chair and continued the vigil over his dying friend.

"I'm glad you're here," Claire said in a soft voice.

"I'm sure Josh is glad you were here." Recalling how she had spoken about her father's illnesses, Neal asked, "Are you a doctor?"

"No, a nurse. Does it show?"

"You seem confident around illness, so yes, I guess it does." Neal smiled at her and again noticed Claire's bulging belly. Conversation had never been his strength and this one could turn into a minefield. *She looks pregnant, but I've seen more than one guy assume that and the woman was just fat. How do I ask? And what about the father? Where is he? Is she even married? Things are so complicated nowadays.* "Ah, you mentioned you live in Everett. Ah, are you … married?"

She grinned. "Yes, I'm married." She rubbed her belly. "Dad would be very perturbed if I wasn't."

His eyes dropped to her belly. "So you're … ah …."

"Pregnant? Yes, that too. Twenty-one weeks."

"So, where is your husband?"

"Rob? He's a lieutenant on the USS *Reagan*. For the last few years, our home has been in Everett."

"Where is he now?"

"Somewhere in the Indian Ocean." Her voice trailed lower with each word and she turned her gaze to the window.

Neal knew what she was thinking. With technology around the world burned out by the sun, what would happen to a modern, computerized vessel? "They harden warships against EMP. He'll come home."

"Could he find me? I didn't leave him a message about where I went."

"He'll figure out where you are." Neal wasn't sure about that and, without autos, Everett and Vancouver were days of travel apart. Minutes passed in silence. Finally, he asked, "It must have been hard watching Josh … your dad, these last few days."

Claire nodded. "He felt okay for the first three days, but these last four have been difficult for both of us. He vomits up anything I try to feed him. He grimaces or shouts in pain, and the last twenty-four hours, he has been in and out of a coma."

More silence passed between them.

Josh's eyes fluttered open and, after a moment, focused on Neal. "Please … get Claire … to a safe place."

"Yes, of course I will." Neal had no idea where a safe place might be or how to get a woman five-months pregnant to such a location, but he felt obliged to commit himself to trying.

Josh smiled and closed his eyes. Over the next several hours, his breathing slowed, became labored, and then stopped.

* * *

King County, Washington, Saturday, September 10th

Conner's legs ached and he needed sleep, but they pedaled south and Madison seemed encouraged as she pointed out trails where she had biked, jogged, or run.

They stopped only when darkness had made it impossible to see. Then, in the twilight before dawn, Madison had awakened and urged him on toward her home.

Several hours later, they entered a hushed Olympia. The lingering cool morning air felt good on Conner's face as he struggled to keep pace with Madison.

The breeze rustled in his ears.

A bird called from a nearby tree.

The quiet of the city rattled his nerves as he waited for the rumble of traffic and machinery that he knew would never come.

Fifty yards ahead, Madison slowed her bike to a stop and stared at the hill before them.

Conner pulled up on her left.

"There." She pointed at the top of the incline. "That's where I live. I can almost see my house." Madison's eyes gleamed with excitement. "We can be there in ten minutes."

Why couldn't your house be at the bottom of the hill? Conner's legs and butt ached, but he smiled weakly.

Madison stared at him for a moment and then she leaned over and kissed him on the lips. "Thank you for getting me home."

Conner grinned at the surprise kiss. He leaned forward to kiss her back, but she had already returned her gaze to the hill.

She had helped him as much as he had helped her, but as Conner's smile grew, he wasn't going to quibble about the details. He didn't want to lose her and so tried to imagine her joy at the reunion with family. He did his best to fix a smile on his face. "Let's climb that hill and get you home."

Engines rumbled in the distance.

Madison led the way to a freeway overpass. As they crossed, half a dozen military and civilian trucks rumbled south along the highway.

Conner stared at the unusual sight. *I wish I could catch a ride with them.*

Several small groups of men and women stared in silence as Madison and Conner pedaled up the hill.

Conner's legs ached as if on a cross-country bike race, but it was only minutes. Finally, Madison stopped and stared at a small, single-story home. "Mom … Dad!" She dismounted, let her bike drop on the grass, and hurried toward the house.

Conner pulled to the front of the home.

She stopped. "The front door is ajar."

Conner slid the rifle into his hand and took the lead as they entered the dark house.

Just inside, Madison stopped and wrinkled her nose. "That smell . . . ."

Conner tried to breathe through his mouth.

Death wafted in the air.

* * *

Rural Lewis County, Washington, Saturday, September 10th

While doing the morning chores, Drake heard the rumble of engines. A week ago, such sounds would have prompted little notice and no concern. Today, it stirred him to hurry his chores and jog down the road with his rifle.

As he rounded a bend, the pastor's home became visible. Just beyond the house and church, a group of men and women stood in the road, watching two bulldozers level ground, clear bushes, and remove small trees along the east side of the hill.

Spotting Pastor Wayne, Drake strode over. As he drew near, another man hurried to the pastor's side. "They're dead. Both of them." After delivering the message, the man hurried away.

"Hi. I didn't think any vehicles worked." The words left Drake's mouth as his mind comprehended the impact of the man's statement.

"Good morning." The pastor smiled at Drake as if no one had just advised him about two deaths. "It's the electronics that are the problem. These old diesel engines don't have any computer chips, electronics, or fuel injection."

Drake had only a vague idea of what fuel injection was, but if not having it helped the dozers work, it must be a good thing. The message of death still echoed in his brain, but no one seemed alarmed so Drake decided to ask later. "What are they doing?" He gestured at the dozers.

"Making a path for the next part of the fence." The pastor pointed to a nearby pile of heavy wooden fence posts and rolled wire.

"Do you have enough fence wire to encircle the hilltop?"

"No." He shook his head. "But we'll go until we run out and then figure some other way to protect the neighborhood."

A man walked up to Pastor Wayne and the two discussed poles, cement, and other fence matters. Drake ambled away, watched the bulldozers for a few minutes, and then returned home. Finding no one in the house, he walked out back. Beside the greenhouse door, Gruff raised his head and wagged his tail.

"Ashley?" Drake called.

She stepped from the greenhouse, trowel in one hand, shotgun in the other. "So, what's all that noise?"

Drake explained about the dozers as he walked across the yard. "What are you doing?"

"Planting a garden." She pointed to a row of pots. "Your father has lots of seeds in that room off of his office. I thought I'd start the plants in here."

"Isn't it late in the year for that?"

"For a lot of plants, yes, but hopefully we'll have enough warm days for a fall garden. We need to start growing food if we're going to live. I was reading." She held up a worn hardcover book. "It was with the seeds. It says you can grow things like broccoli, kale, chard, and carrots this time of year."

Drake shook his head. "I hate broccoli, don't know what chard or kale is, and carrots are just okay."

"We can eat them if we're hungry or trade them for things we need."

Of course, she was right. They would need to grow whatever food they could, both for eating and trade. Once again, Drake felt stupid for not realizing their value earlier. For the next couple of hours, the dozers rumbled in the background while Drake worked alongside Ashley to plant seeds.

Out in the garden area beside the greenhouse, Ashley wiped sweat from her forehead. "Are the bulldozers getting closer?"

"They might be." Drake pushed his shovel into the soft ground. "They're going to run the security fence along the back of our property."

Ashley grinned at Drake but said nothing.

Drake's face burned as he thought about what he had said. Had he implied a relationship? He wanted her as a girlfriend and more, but they were just fifteen. Did their age even matter anymore? Was this their place now? Would he and Ashley just continue on until—?

Gruff barked.

"Hi, Pastor Wayne!" Ashley waved as the preacher strode across the orchard. "Is everything all right?"

"Everything is as good as it can be." The pastor looked at Drake. "The fence crew is near the back of your property. Would you like to join us?"

"Yes, I would." Drake turned to Ashley. "If you'll be okay?"

She nodded. "I've got Gruff and the shotgun."

As Drake gathered a posthole digger, shovels, and fence tools into a wheelbarrow, he repeatedly peeked at Ashley. Probably they had both lost family, but having her here gave him a sense of comfort. He grinned and hoped she also felt comforted.

"Ready to go?" Pastor Wayne asked.

"Oh … yeah." Drake nodded.

As they crossed the orchard out of earshot from Ashley, Drake turned to him. "This morning just before I talked with you, another guy came up and … what did he mean when he said, 'They're dead. Both of them'?"

Pastor Wayne drew in a deep breath.

Drake maneuvered the wheelbarrow along the path behind the preacher. "So, who died?"

The two walked along in silence for a moment. "Have you wondered why you haven't been scheduled for sentry duty?"

"No." Drake shook his head. "I figured you just hadn't gotten to me yet."

"I took your name off the list."

"Why?"

"The sentries have been attacked a couple of times." Pastor Wayne opened a gate to a field of cornstalks. "I didn't want to put you in danger."

Drake followed him through and closed the gate. "Are you saying that two of the sentries were killed?"

"Yes." The pastor sighed. "A couple that lived down the road from your friend Ashley. They didn't check in this morning. We found their bodies along the north side path."

"You might have taken my name off a list, but I think I'm still in danger. We all are."

Pastor Wayne nodded and pointed to the men building the fence a hundred yards ahead. "Hopefully, this will help."

"How much of the fence has been finished?"

"Less than half."

Day eight

Clark County, Washington, Sunday, September 11th

Grateful for the gray sky and cool breeze, Neal pulled the gloves from his sore hands and popped blisters with a pocketknife. Rarely had he thought about the difficulties of digging a grave with just a pick-and-shovel. The effort had proven to be especially hard in this clay soil. They were always six-feet deep in the movies, but he had dug maybe four and his hands were stiff and ached.

Ginger lay on the grass nearby and watched.

Never had he thought of digging a grave in a backyard. The idea of burying Josh in the shallow, oblong hole that he had managed to dig seemed so disrespectful. He slammed the pick into the hard ground and pain radiated once again from a half dozen blisters. The compromise came at five-feet, a depth that showed respect but would leave Neal with enough strength to carry Josh to it and cover him with the earth.

Neal struggled to lift himself from the hole with heavy arms and weak hands. After several tries, he rolled onto the grass. For a moment, he lay there staring up at dark clouds.

Ginger licked his face.

"Stop it." Neal rolled to a sitting position and scratched Ginger's neck and ears.

Claire stepped out the back door. "I wrapped Dad in a sheet as best I could."

"I'm sure it's fine." He stood and rubbed his arms.

After water and rest, Neal hoisted the dead weight of his friend and, with stumbles and sways, managed to carry Josh's body to the graveside.

Claire sobbed as Neal slid into the hole with her shrouded father. Then, with an awkward thud, Neal laid his friend to rest.

Neal climbed out and stood. "Fair winds and following seas, my friend. I believe you're in a better place."

"Dad is in the best place." Claire closed her eyes. "Lord, You tell us that neither death nor life, angels, demons, powers, height or depth ... that nothing can separate us from Your love. I know that You prepared a place for my dad and that he is with You now, so I'm not going to let my heart be troubled. Thank You, Lord, for such a good father. Please bring Rob back to me." She stood in silence for several moments. "Goodbye, Dad." With her head down, she retreated to the porch and sat.

Neal pushed the shovel into the piled earth and covered Josh. As he finished, the sky opened up with rain. "Come." He called to Ginger and then walked past Claire on the porch. "I'm done and going inside."

Claire followed.

In the living room, Neal pulled dry but dirty clothes from his pack and sniffed them. "These smell bad. I wish I could wash them—and bathe."

"We have cold water. Dad collected rainwater from the roof into barrels for his garden." Claire looked out the window toward the grave in the back. "But, I wouldn't wash your clothes. It's raining."

Neal raised a confused eyebrow.

"Your clothes won't dry overnight in this humidity." She turned her gaze to the stairs. "But, you could use some of the water for a bath and I can find you some of Dad's clothes."

"That would be nice."

Neal carried two buckets of cold rainwater to the bathtub. Standing in the tub, he closed the drain and poured one bucket over his head. After a gasp and shiver, he soaped himself down and poured the second bucket over his head. Then he used the water in the tub to scrub the dirty or soapy spots he had missed.

Neal stepped from the tub of gray water. He shivered again as he toweled off. Painful hands moved him to check the medicine cabinet for a first-aid kit. Finding one, he used the topical antibiotic on the multiple blisters that dotted his hands. Then he wrapped them both in bandages.

Downstairs, Ginger gave him an odd look. Neal wondered if he smelled different. Walking into the dining room, he found Claire rubbing her hair with a towel. "Using some of that rainwater to wash your hair?"

"I might as well." She shrugged. "The barrels are full and it's still raining."

"I think we should rest tonight." Neal sat across the table from her. "Then, if it isn't raining in the morning, we should go."

"Go?"

"To my farm outside of Riverbank. It's the safest place I know."

"I'm staying here until my husband returns."

"You heard your father. He wants you in a safe place. Here, alone, with a baby coming, that's not safe."

"You said Rob would figure it out and come here and I'm going to wait until he does."

"And what if he's …."

Neal silenced himself, but Claire's angry eyes revealed that she knew his meaning.

"Dead? Then this is my home."

"I'm not staying here and your father asked me to take you to a safe place. Do you want to have the baby all alone?"

"No, but women have had babies alone before."

"And many have died alone." Neal shook his head. "You need to come with me. Riverbank is at least closer to your home and I know people there who can help deliver the baby."

Her angry expression softened. "It is closer to our home in Everett. You know a midwife?"

Neal didn't know a midwife or anyone else with real experience in delivering babies, but he needed to persuade her to accompany him. "Yes. Police and firefighters. I know several." *Well, I handle their taxes and investments.*

"But what if Rob comes here?"

"Hopefully we could leave word for him either when he reached Riverbank or before, but if he did get here, we could paint a message for him on a wall. Do you know your neighbors?"

"A few. Why?"

"We'll tell them also."

Claire nodded.

"Then we agree? We'll leave for Riverbank in the morning, right?"

"How soon could we get there?"

"Let's see … tomorrow is Monday. If we start early, we could reach Riverbank by Tuesday evening."

Claire stared out a window at the grave of her father and then nodded slowly.

* * *

King County, Washington, Sunday, September 11th

"Stay back." Afraid that the stench drifted from her dead parents, Conner didn't want Madison to see. He also didn't want to smell it and tried not to breathe as he inched deeper into the house with his rifle ready.

The smell grew stronger as he crossed the house. "What rooms are ahead?" He glanced back over his shoulder.

Still by the front door, Madison looked ready to cry. "The kitchen and dining room."

Conner edged forward and turned to his left at the next entryway. He gasped at the sight of a dead man on the dining room floor, surrounded by dark dry blood.

"What!" Madison ran forward.

Conner tried to stop her, but she struggled past him.

She gasped then looked again. "Who's that?"

"I thought it might be your father."

"No." She turned away. "He is … was too young and I think he … ah, was Hispanic."

Conner coughed. "We can figure this out in the fresh air." He turned to leave.

A man with a baseball bat stood just inside the door. Most of his face was covered by a scarf.

Madison gasped. "Mr. Winters … Arnold … is that you?"

He pulled down the scarf, revealing several days' growth of a gray stubble beard. "Madison?"

Before he could say another word, she asked, "Where are Mom and Dad?"

He shook his head and pointed toward the room with the body. "Your dad said that guy broke in, acting all crazy. Tom fought with him—"

"Who's Tom?" Conner asked.

"Who are you?" Winters asked.

"Stop it!" Madison shouted. "Tom is my father; Maria is my mother's name." She focused on Winters. "Where are Mom and Dad?"

"That's what I was saying. The crazy guy and your dad fought and while they struggled Roxie bit him ... the dead guy ... and must have cut an artery. He died in no time."

Conner figured Roxie was a dog but decided not to ask.

Madison's jaw clenched for a moment. "Where's Dad? Is he okay? Where's Mom?"

"Oh, yeah." He nodded. "Your dad's okay. A little bruised and shook up."

"Where is he?"

"He went with your mom to the hospital."

"Why?"

"After all the commotion, fighting, and dying, your mom collapsed ... couldn't talk right and had trouble seeing."

"What?"

"Your dad borrowed my bike and cart to take her there." He shook his head. "That was three days ago. He hasn't come back with my bike."

"Next time, if there is a next time, start with that." Madison ran toward the door.

"About my bike?"

"Where are you going?" Conner dashed to catch up with her.

"The hospital," she said without pausing. "It's only a mile away."

She grabbed her bike and darted toward her destination.

Conner followed, trying to keep up. Within a few minutes, he spotted the eleven-story main building. Conner slowed to a stop as he stared at the modern structure surrounded by large cedar trees. This was the place they had all hurried to that horrible night someone mugged and knifed his mother.

They had arrived too late. She was gone.

"Come on!" Madison pointed. "That's the hospital. We're almost there."

Conner forced himself to pedal onward as memories of his mother, and the days of tears that followed her death, surged from the dark recesses of his mind.

"I'll need to take your rifle."

"Huh?" Conner asked the soldier in front of him.

"You'll get it back when you leave," a sentry said flatly. "But no weapons are allowed inside the perimeter. What's your full name?"

"Conner … Conner Evans." As he spoke, he became aware of several nearby tents with soldiers and doctors hurrying about. Madison stood next to a big Red Cross sign, talking to a woman. Several large generators roared at the far end of the parking lot. A line of green army trucks spewed diesel fumes as they left through a gate just feet away.

The sentry wrote Conner's name on a tag and handed the rifle to another soldier. "Do you have any other weapons?"

Conner handed him the pistol and then pushed on with his bike toward Madison.

She waved him onward. "The Red Cross is helping families find each other." Madison pointed to a nearby table. "We can check for admissions and discharges there." She took a clipboard labeled, "Admissions."

"Ah, Croft is your last name, right?"

Without looking up from the papers, Madison nodded.

Conner grabbed the discharge list and scanned the pages until he spotted both.

Tom Croft, deceased.

Maria Croft, deceased.

He stared at the page. How had both her parents died? How would he tell Madison?

She flipped to another page and leaned close. "Both of them were admitted to the hospital." She looked to Conner. "Why would both be admitted?"

"Ah … I …." What could he say to make this easier for her?"

"What?" Her mouth hung open. She stared and slowly held out her hand.

Perhaps it was best for her to read the words herself. He passed the clipboard.

She scanned the page. "No!" She sank to her knees "Why? How?"

Conner knelt, hugged her, and eased her back to her feet as the Red Cross woman ran over.

Between tears, Madison repeated various combinations of how, why, and pointed to the clipboard.

Conner explained the situation to the woman.

"I'll find out what I can." The woman hurried to the tent.

After a few minutes, Conner led Madison to the shade of a nearby tree. Through teary eyes, Madison kept watch for the woman as, over the next hour, her tears subsided to sniffles.

After more minutes of sad silence, the woman left the tent. Carrying a clipboard and plastic bag, she walked toward them. Conner stood. Madison did the same and clutched Conner's hand.

"I don't have much information. Everyone is just trying to keep things going until the electricity is back on. Ah … your father was admitted at the same time as your mother." She glanced at the papers in her hand. "He had symptoms of a heart attack and passed away about an hour after admission."

Madison bit her lip and seemed ready to cry again.

"Your mother had repeated strokes and passed away the next morning. I'm very sorry."

"No. I don't believe it." Madison shook her head. "How could two healthy people just die like that?"

"Sometimes these things happen."

"I need to bury them."

The woman cringed. "I'm really very sorry, but any unclaimed bodies are buried in a mass grave within twenty-four hours. I am so sorry." She held out the plastic bag. Madison took it and the woman hurried away.

"Their wedding rings." Madison said, looking through the bag. "My dad's wallet." She slid to the ground in tears.

Conner sat beside her. He let her cry and held back tears of his own. When she gulped in deep breaths, he realized she had stopped weeping. Then he retrieved his weapons and they left on their bikes.

Just outside the perimeter fence, Madison stopped. "Where am I going?"

Conner felt thoroughly confused. "Home."

"My parent's home? Is it home now with both of them dead and a body in the dining room? How could I live there ever again? Where will I go? Back to college? Is it even open?"

Conner stared at her, searching for an answer to at least one of her questions, but he had none. Until this day, his goal had been much the same as Madison's—get home. He had no idea what he would do if he arrived at the farm and found Drake dead. He hadn't wanted to spend the weekend babysitting his little brother, but he should have been there. Guilt surged within him. Had his father made it home? Would Madison go to the farm with him? Should he even ask her?

"That's the bike!" Madison ran to a man standing beside a "For Trade" sign. Around him were a couple of bicycles, wagons, assorted MREs, and canned goods in cardboard boxes. "That's my friend's bike. You stole it!" Madison thrust her finger in the direction of a newer bike with a four-foot trailer.

"I didn't steal nothing." The man jumped between her and the bike.

Madison edged closer. "Yes, you did!"

Conner shook his head in disbelief. Why did she care so much about this?

Madison grabbed at the bike.

The man pushed her away.

Afraid that she would start a fight, or worse, get herself killed, Conner spoke. "I'll trade you for it."

"What'ya got?"

Conner pulled his backpack off and opened it. He didn't have much, a tarp, sleeping bag, a canteen and some matches. Then he pulled the pistol from his pocket. "This for the bicycle and the trailer."

The man smiled. "Good trade. I'll swap you another bike for that rifle on your shoulder."

"No." Conner handed him the pistol and, with a bike on either side of him, walked to Madison. "Are you okay?"

She nodded.

Glad that Madison had calmed down, Conner put his bike in the trailer of Arnold's and the two biked toward her home. "You can go faster. Go ahead. I'll catch up."

"No." She shook her head. "There's no hurry. There's no place I need to be."

Tears occasionally rolled down Madison's cheeks, but no words passed her lips until they neared her parent's home. "You traded for the bike, but can I give it back to Arnold?"

"Sure."

She sped past her house, climbed the steps to Arnold's porch, and banged on his door.

Arnold opened it with a smile. "You brought my bike back!" Still staring at the bike, he asked, "Is your mom okay? Is your dad here?"

"No!" Madison shouted. Tears erupted and she ran into her parents' house, slamming the front door behind her.

Conner turned to Arnold. "Her mom and dad are dead, but she wanted you to have the bike back. I'm not really sure why."

Conner left Arnold's bike and trailer and joined Madison, who had exited her parents' home and sat on the front porch. He sat with her in silence, unsure of what to do or say.

Madison turned to him with a weak smile. "Thank you for helping me get home."

"I wish it had been a happier homecoming."

She stared at the house over her shoulder. "There's nothing left for me here."

More silence passed between them as Conner mustered his courage. "Earlier you were wondering where home is. You're welcome to come with me to the farm. I've really gotten to like you. I'm not saying we have to—"

"Yes."

The word had been a whisper. Had he really heard it? He stared at her for confirmation.

"I'll go with you."

* * *

Rural Lewis County, Washington, Sunday, September 11th

Drake watched as Pastor Wayne pulled the ancient rope to ring the bell high in the steeple of the old brick church. Drake sat in the front pew and stared at his sore and blistered hands. Over the weekend, he had worked with neighbors to extend the fence past his property. He hoped that it helped, but the fence ended a hundred yards beyond his place. The bad guys could just walk around it.

Pastor Wayne and Michael, the ornery old farmer he had met four days ago, walked to the front of the sanctuary, talking about harvesting food from nearby fields.

"Anyway, that was a good service this morning," Michael said.

"You should come more often."

Michael laughed. "Maybe I should." Then he walked away.

Dozens soon arrived for the community meeting. Drake lost count and restarted at the back with a slow walk forward toward Pastor Wayne.

"You're doing Sunday services?" Gail rocked the baby in her arms.

"I never stopped. Nine every Sunday morning." Pastor Wayne smiled at the baby. "How are—"

Sixty-eight. "You should ring the bell for services, like in the old days," Drake said.

Pastor Wayne rubbed his chin. "I should." He looked around. "Where did Gail go?"

Drake looked for the woman with the baby. The sanctuary was fuller than he had ever seen it. He shrugged. "I don't see her or the crazy guy she lives with."

Max, the beekeeper, stepped over to the preacher. "We're ready to start."

Pastor Wayne nodded and stepped onto the podium. "Good evening, everyone. We wanted to talk about how the fence project is going and about the food and water problems."

"The fence stops hundreds of yards before my place," a man in the back yelled. "It isn't going to keep anyone out."

"Where can we get water?" a woman shouted. "I've been using a stream."

Pastor Wayne held up a hand. "We can figure it out if we work together."

Outside the church, an engine rumbled.

Silence fell on those inside. Drake and several others ran out to investigate.

A Humvee pulled into the church parking lot and parked. Deputy Campbell stepped from the vehicle. "I heard the bell and figured you were having another meeting."

"Do you have news?" a man asked.

Campbell sighed. "Yeah, I've got some."

The group surrounded the deputy and ushered him to the front of the church.

Pastor Wayne shook Campbell's hand and then stepped aside.

"Well, I'm afraid this is a good news, bad news day," the deputy started.

Calls for the good news mixed with an audible groan that swept the sanctuary.

"You people on Fremont Hill have done well in getting organized. Reports of gang activity here and in Riverbank are down."

"I'm guessing that's the good news," someone shouted. "What's the bad?"

"The gangs seem to be gaining members and growing bolder. Don't travel outside of the Riverbank and Fremont Hill areas. They have roadblocks along the freeway and state highway both to the north and south."

Day nine

Clark County, Washington, Monday, September 12th

While he waited for Claire to catch up, Neal leaned against an abandoned red Corvette. He pulled on the door handle, but it didn't open and no keys were in the ignition. A low grumble of irritation escaped from him. With this car he could have been home in less than an hour. Neal pulled his shoe off a sore and blistered foot.

Ginger sniffed the shoe but turned her nose away and pawed at Neal's backpack.

"I'll feed you later." Neal took several gulps of water and then squirted some into his hand for Ginger.

As the dog lapped at the water, Neal watched Claire shuffle closer. *At this rate, her husband might reach Riverbank before we do.*

He shook his head. *Don't be mean.*

Neal mustered his patience and fixed a smile on his face.

Despite being fifteen or so years younger, pregnancy slowed Claire more than age and blisters slowed him. Well, the backpack and sleeping bag she carried reduced her pace, but what could he do? She had insisted on carrying them.

That morning, before they departed, Claire had visited several neighbors and told them where she would be. Neal painted a similar message, including his address, on the living room wall. If Claire's husband searched, he would know where to go.

He envied the love she had for her husband and the new life she would soon bring into the world. Neal once had that with Beth—years ago.

The conference in Vegas had been an escape. A means of avoiding painful memories. A reprieve from his teenage sons.

But now, reaching home filled his waking moments. *Please God, let them be okay.*

He hated his irritation with Claire's ponderous pace. He understood that pregnancy caused it, but he was so close to home. Even at this slow rate, they might reach Riverbank by tomorrow evening, but each mile closer made him more eager to complete the journey.

Claire ambled to the Corvette, leaned against it, and drank some water. "Are we still on schedule?"

No! Neal continued to smile. "Sure, we'll reach it tomorrow sometime."

"You know, the constant smile on your face is a little creepy."

"Oh, sorry." The grin faded as Neal felt his face flush and turned away.

"Am I slowing you down?"

Neal sighed and looked back at Claire. "I don't know but not that much. It's really about me." He explained both his guilt at leaving for the conference and his wish now to return home to his sons.

"I'll pray for all of you." She stepped forward. "Come on, Ginger, let's lead the way."

They continued north along the freeway. Claire led for a mile, then Neal overtook her, but he slowed down and walked beside her for the rest of the day.

Hours later, when they reached Longview, sunlight cast long shadows over an otherwise dark town.

"Do you want to camp for the night?" Claire asked.

Neal didn't want to stop, but he perched on the freeway's center divider. "Sure, let's find a place to camp."

Claire pointed to a small park beside the freeway where clusters of tents stood and several campfires glowed.

"I haven't had the best of luck with other people." He looked for another option. "I prefer to be alone."

"Being alone isn't an option anymore." Claire trudged toward the off ramp. "You've got me with you now and I can't walk much farther."

"Females," Neal muttered and stared at Ginger. He recalled how the dog had insisted on coming with him. "Claire's made up her mind so we better get moving."

Neal and Ginger followed her into the camp.

Several dozen tents and campfires marked the site that spread along the east bank of the Cowlitz River. No one seemed to pay much attention to Neal, Claire, or Ginger as they strolled along, looking for a place to sleep.

"There." Neal pointed to a large evergreen tree with two waist-high boulders to one side. "It'll give us some protection if it rains and the nearby rocks will provide cover in case of gunfire."

Claire stared at him for a moment. "Has anyone ever called you paranoid?"

"Yes."

"Okay, just checking. Let's sleep there." Claire helped him spread the tarps and sleeping bags on the ground between the rocks and trees.

Neal fed Ginger the last of the dog food while Claire ate soup from home. Together they shared an MRE.

"That's the last of the food." Neal handed Claire a packet of crackers.

"We'll reach your farm sometime tomorrow, right?"

"Yes." Neal licked his fingers. "I'd guess in the late afternoon if all goes well."

As darkness filled the air, Neal lay on the ground, trying to sleep. Ginger slept nearby, exhaling dog breath across his face. Thoughts of home mixed with food. He tossed and turned on his side.

A few feet away, Claire shifted and started snoring.

He sat up, wishing he had a good book or newspaper to read. Nearby, five men gathered around a fire pit. They seemed like average guys. Two were overweight. All were a bit flabby. None appeared to be armed. Neal walked over and joined them.

A man in his thirties nodded as he approached. "As I was saying, I was in Salem when the sun storm happened." He shook his head. "I almost got killed going through Portland. People are desperate for food." He knelt and held his hands close to the fire.

Neal squatted and warmed his hands.

"I'm trying to reach my family in Seattle," the man continued. "But the way is blocked."

Neal looked to the man. "Blocked? What do you mean?"

"You haven't heard?" He shook his head. "Bandits are killing and looting between here and Riverbank."

* * *

Olympia, Washington, Monday, September 12th

Conner plopped a cardboard box into the trailer behind Arnold's bike. "Any more stuff?" he called to Madison.

"Just this suitcase." Madison stepped from the front door and stared at the house. "How did you get Arnold to give you the bike and trailer?" She set the case in the trailer.

Fearing that she might not appreciate what he had done, Conner hesitated to explain. "Well … you said you were taking everything you wanted, right?"

She nodded.

"First, I offered him my bike for his, but that wasn't enough to convince him, so I said he could have any pieces of furniture in the house that he wanted."

"We're leaving. In a few minutes, he could take anything he wants."

"Yeah, but he won't know that we've left until he gets dressed and walks over here."

With sad eyes, she stared at the house for several moments, and then she turned to Conner. "We'd better go."

Conner imagined the feelings that must be stabbing her heart. Both parents were dead and this would never be her home again. In one week, the foundations of her world had crumbled.

He thought of his father and brother. He hoped that any change in his future wouldn't be as drastic or sudden as the trauma she had suffered.

As the sun rose, warming the day, they biked south along the freeway. All the vehicles had been pushed to the side of the highway, clearing the center for easy travel.

Madison led the way with her long, brunette hair flowing in the breeze. Riding the trailer bike, Conner pushed to keep within shouting distance.

Near noon, Madison rolled down a small hill and stopped.

Conner wiped perspiration from his forehead as he stopped alongside her. "Are you tired?"

"No. Do you want me to ride the trailer bike for a while?"

"I'm fine." He struggled to breathe, slow and even.

"When do you think we'll reach Riverbank?"

"We're making good time." Conner shrugged. "Maybe two more hours."

They continued over the next hill and down a flat area of fields and farms. Conner paused by a stream and splashed water on his face.

Madison continued up the forested slope. Near the top, she stopped and dismounted her bike.

Did she have a flat or did the bike break down?

She stood beside the bike and stared at the gravel edge of the road.

Pedaling hard, Conner neared her in seconds. "Is something wrong?"

Madison pointed to a man sprawled facedown beside the road.

The sound of distant voices carried on the wind.

Conner dismounted, ran over, and gently shook the man's arm. "Are you okay?"

"Is he dead?" Madison whispered.

"I don't know yet." Conner pulled back the collar and pressed two fingers against his neck. The skin felt warm, but he found no pulse. He rolled the body over. Red blood stained the front of the shirt around a single bullet wound. "Yeah, I think he's dead."

Madison walked a few yards toward the top of the hill. She stopped near the crest, bent low, and peered over.

"What are you doing?" Conner asked.

She scurried back to him and in a voice laced with fear whispered, "Guys with guns are coming."

Conner heard men talking. He grabbed his bike and motioned for Madison to follow him into the forest.

Conner found a gully where a creek flowed and motioned for Madison to stay there with the bikes. Then he moved to the side and found a spot where he could watch the road.

"There's the guy I shot." A tall man with shaggy brown hair strode along the freeway. "See, I told you he wouldn't get far."

Behind shrubs and trees, Conner held his breath.

A second man with short black hair and a goatee stepped close to the corpse. "Shoot better next time." He looked around. "I thought I heard someone talking."

"Probably just him dying," Shaggy said.

"Maybe." Goatee continued to look around. "Hide the body in the forest so it doesn't warn the next traveler, and then hightail it back to camp." He turned and strode away.

"How come I always get this kind of job?" Shaggy stared down for a moment then grabbed each arm of the body and pulled it off the road, across the drainage ditch, and into the woods nearby.

Conner barely breathed as he inched around a large evergreen tree to conceal himself.

Shaggy dragged the body inches from the tree.

When he had passed, Conner crept back to the creek where Madison hid with the bikes. He kept low and pointed his rifle in the direction of Shaggy's noisy trek. Conner caught glimpses as the man left the body and strolled from the forest to the asphalt highway and disappeared.

"I think we're okay now." Conner took a deep breath. "I'm glad you spotted those guys."

"What do we do now?"

"I'm sure we can get around them, but before we go anywhere, I want to know exactly where they are."

"No, let's just go back to Olympia."

The words hit Conner like a slap in the face. He didn't want to lose her. "If you want to, you can but … I've got to find out if my brother and father are okay."

Madison stared at the ground for several moments. "I understand. I'll stay with you, but I don't want … I couldn't take it if you died or were killed like that poor man beside the road."

Conner hugged her. "I'll be careful."

She wrapped her arms around his shoulder and neck. "You better." She kissed him.

He squeezed her tighter and for a moment the horrid events of the last few days faded. He kissed her back.

* * *

From his vantage point atop a nearby hill, Conner watched as bikers on two black motorcycles led three 1950s-era pickups up to a home near the freeway ramp. Conner didn't know much about motorcycles, but the style of these two looked as old as the trucks.

The newer, two-story white house appeared to serve as the gang's headquarters. Earlier he had spotted both Goatee and Shaggy, along with about ten other men and three women. More were probably inside. In the quiet that had become normal, he had heard some of their words but learned nothing useful.

As men unloaded boxes from the back of the trucks, a third biker in dark leather roared up to the house on a red motorcycle. Over his shoulder, he wore a satchel, like a messenger. When he dismounted, he pulled goggles up from his eyes.

Conner glanced north, toward where he had left Madison. He wanted to return to her, but they would need a plan to circumvent these thugs. He pulled the map from his pack and searched for the best route.

Nearby, male voices spoke in whispers.

Twigs snapped.

Conner turned in the direction of the voices and froze. A wolf stared at him from not ten feet away.

In an unhurried back-and-forth sway, the animal shifted its gaze from Conner to the oncoming voices.

Moving slowly and holding his breath, Conner reached for his rifle.

The beast snarled.

With his arm in midreach, Conner stopped.

The wolf gazed into the forest for several moments. Then four pups edged out of the shadows. Together they hurried away into the forest.

Conner sighed with relief, but the voices remained and seemed closer. Taking another slow, deep breath, he eased himself into nearby shrubs. Moments later, Shaggy and two other men strode from the forest and crossed where the wolves had been moments earlier.

"I saw a wolf, I tell you." Shaggy gestured ahead of him. "It must have come through here."

"The boss wants us to find Danny. Not an overgrown dog."

Holding still, Conner waited for them to pass. When they had gone, he slipped from his hiding place and crept several hundred yards.

More twigs snapped.

Another wolf or more men? Conner slid into a grove of large fir trees. Wolves might be less dangerous.

Two more unfamiliar voices whispered as they passed him in the darkness.

"Where do you think the girl is going?" one man whispered.

"I don't know. Let's just find Danny and get back to the house."

Conner inched a few yards to the gully and hid along the bank. He listened for the slightest sound. Hearing nothing, he eased forward.

Cigarette smoke wafted on the breeze.

He waited and watched a red glow float by a few yards distant.

For the next several hours, men in groups of two or three moved through the forest in a noisy and apparently haphazard search for the girl and Danny. Why didn't they call for them? Did they run away? Escape? If they were looking for someone who escaped, why were some smoking or talking? Even if they whispered, it seemed really thoughtless. If they were stupid, Conner was grateful. It increased his chances of avoiding them.

But progress remained slow, and eventually, the darkness of the forest grew so deep that he couldn't see the trees in front of him. Crawling into shrubs that he hoped would hide him for the night, he prayed for Madison's safety and waited for sunrise.

Day ten

Clark County, Washington, Tuesday, September 13th

As the sun rose on a new day, Neal leaned against a boulder, thinking of eggs and bacon.

Ginger sniffed and pawed at the backpack.

Claire grunted, rolled on her side, and opened her eyes. "Coffee would be so good right now."

"That would be nice." He added it to his imaginary breakfast. "But we don't have any coffee or food and we have another problem." Neal relayed the news about bandits that he had learned during the night

Claire moaned and struggled to a sitting position. "But we can go around them, can't we?"

"Sure, but it will take longer."

"Everything seems to be taking longer." Claire used a low limb to pull herself up. "No coffee, no food." She shook her head. "Let's get started."

Hours later, Neal wiped his brow with a sleeve and then looked into the blue sky. For most of the day, they hiked slowly north in a wide arc toward Riverbank. It had been a warm day. A few clouds would have been nice, but as the sun passed its zenith and slipped toward the horizon, Neal longed to be home. "Are you tired?"

"A bit."

"We can stop if you need to, but the farm is—"

"I can go on."

Neal smiled, thankful for her endurance. "We should be there about nightfall."

*　　*　　*

Thurston County, Washington, Tuesday, September 13th

Birds twittered in the predawn twilight as Conner inched through the forest, listening for any threat.

Leaves rustled with the breeze.

Using hills and trees as cover, he wound his way back toward the gully where he left Madison. When he spotted her, he dashed the last twenty yards and slid down the slope beside her.

She slammed a fist into his groin and with the other hand swung a rock at his face. She stopped with a gasp. "Conner! What were you thinking, coming up on me like that? I could have killed you! Where have you been? I was so worried."

Conner held up a finger, signaling her to wait as pain radiated from his groin. A few minutes later, as it subsided, he inhaled a deep breath. "Hitting below the belt is against the rules."

"Sorry," she said in a soft voice. "Where were you?"

"Hiding and trying not to get killed." Conner described his night. "The gang is looking for someone named Danny and a girl. They might have been lost, but the thugs didn't call for them. I think the two might be trying to escape."

"You may be right." Madison frowned. "They're probably on the run from those killers. I feel sorry for them."

"Feel sorry for us." Conner shook his head. "We'll need to avoid their searches." He pulled out his map. "The gang will look close to their base. Let's go back a couple of exits and cross over to here." He pointed out the route with a finger.

Madison nodded.

Conner did a quick check of the area and spotted no one.

"The searchers probably have moved farther away." He grabbed the trailer bike. "We need to be careful. I'll stay in the lead."

She nodded and they both walked out to the highway and then sped away on their bikes. After retracing their route north for two miles, they exited the freeway and turned south toward Riverbank.

Later, Conner spotted an abandoned gravel pit where he and his friends had gone swimming on hot summer evenings. He paused to splash the cool water on his face.

Madison rolled to a stop beside him. "This is taking a lot longer." She gulped water from a canteen.

"Yeah, but I don't think Goatee, Shaggy, and the others have followed us, so I'm happy." He looked at the map. "We're coming in a back way."

"Is that a problem?"

"No, not really." Conner shook his head. "We'll be on winding back lanes all the way to the farm. Since I know these roads, I want to stay in the lead. I could find my way home from here in pitch blackness." He looked into the sky. *And we'll probably get to the farm after nightfall.*

"Do we have any food left?" Madison asked.

"No." Suddenly anxious to see home, Conner said, "Let's get going."

Several hours later, long shadows shaded the roads. Still, sweat rolled down Conner's forehead, burning his eyes. He squinted and blinked as he struggled to read the sign ahead. Then he wiped his face with a sleeve and the words snapped into clear view. Braking to a stop, he pointed. "Entering Lewis County! This is where I live." He grinned, remounted his bike, and sped south as fast as he could.

Madison pulled alongside and smiled.

For the next few minutes, they pedaled side by side down the quiet country road. He watched her pull strands of long brunette hair as it flapped into her face as she pedaled beside him. They had been through a lot, but together they had found a way to survive. He wanted to somehow express those feelings to her. If he could just find—

Madison looked back. "What's that noise?"

"A motorcycle!" Conner motioned toward the woods. "Quick, follow me."

They were barely off the road when a biker, wearing goggles and carrying a satchel, roared around the corner on an old red Harley.

Conner reached for the rifle slung over his shoulder.

The biker slowed, waved a pistol, and shook his head. He gazed intently at both Conner and Madison before he revved the bike and disappeared around the next bend.

"I saw that guy." Conner wiped his face with both hands.

"Where?" Madison asked as they walked back to the road.

"At that house with the other gang members. He drove up while I was watching. I think he's some kind of messenger."

"I'm glad he wasn't interested in us."

A shot boomed.

Madison frowned. "Maybe he was interested in someone else."

"Maybe."

The roar of the motorcycle engine faded into the distance.

Conner mounted his bike. "I'll lead." He had learned to drive along many of these back roads and had traveled most of them in the years since. Less than a mile ahead, he eased his bike into sharp curve. Images of twisted metal, blood, and death flashed in his mind. Deadman's Curve. Several head-on collisions had occurred in the bend, and at other times drivers slid and hit the bridge.

The bridge. He took a deep breath as unwanted memories raced into his mind. A few months after obtaining his license, he had followed a friend's car around this curve. The friend had gone too fast, slid on wet pavement, and bashed into the narrow bridge with a metal ripping roar he would never forget. Slamming on the brakes, Conner's car slid toward the mangled vehicle but stopped inches away. He lived, but his friend didn't.

Most locals took the curve slowly. Conner coasted slowly around the curve on his bike.

He saw the bridge first, then the leather-clad biker, sprawled face up in the middle of the road nearby.

Conner braked and dismounted his bike.

Madison gasped.

He waved for her to back away and then he gazed along the trees for bandits.

Birds chirped.

Seeing no threat, Conner eased forward and, for the second time in two days, pressed fingers against the neck of a dead man. A single bullet wound marred his chest. Deep shadows now covered parts of the road. The biker may not have even seen the person who killed him.

His goggles and satchel were gone, probably snatched by whoever stole the red Harley.

"Is he dead?" Madison asked weakly.

"Yeah." Conner nodded. "We probably should get away from here."

As the sun continued its downward trek, Conner and Madison hurried south into the growing darkness.

* * *

Rural Lewis County, Washington, Tuesday, September 13th

Neal felt every year of his age in aching legs and sore feet. As the sun fell below the horizon, filling the world with shadows, he and Claire stopped to rest. Now he struggled with the idea of continuing on. If he did, they could reach the farm in a couple of hours. He forced his tired body to move.

In the distance, the sound of a motorcycle grew.

"Do you hear that?" Claire asked.

Neal nodded. With both the shadows of late evening and the distance they were from the road, it seemed unlikely anyone speeding by on a motorcycle would notice them, but Neal eased the shotgun onto his lap as he listened and waited for the biker to pass.

He braced himself as the engine's roar grew louder.

Tires and brakes squealed.

Silence reclaimed the night.

Neal held his breath. What had happened? An accident? Ambush?

Angry shouts and curses from a woman quickly shattered the stillness.

Holding his shotgun, Neal rose to his feet and handed the leash to Claire. "Stay here. I'll check it out."

"I'll be right behind you."

Neal grunted. "Okay." He trudged along the shoulder of the road, staying close to the trees.

Around the next bend in the road, a woman with dark hair waved a flashlight as she kicked and cursed at a red Harley lying on the pavement. She stormed away from the bike and then back toward it, shook her head, and cursed some more.

Neal pointed the shotgun in her direction. "Having problems with the bike?"

She spun around with a pistol in one hand, goggles and flashlight in the other.

"I heard you and came to investigate. I didn't mean to startle you." He squinted through the light, trying to look at her but saw only short dark hair, dark jacket, and jeans.

Claire stepped from the tree line.

Ginger growled.

She stared at the dog for a moment and then at Claire. Slowly she eased the gun and flashlight down. "Sorry. A girl can't be too careful these days."

"My name's Neal." He lowered his weapon. "What's wrong?"

"Danny." She stared at the bike for a moment.

Confused by the name, Neal glanced about.

"No. I'm Dani, with an 'i.' As for the bike, I don't know. I hit a pothole and blew the tire, but now it won't even start." She kicked the bike again. "I know how to fix these things, but it's so dark and I've got no tools with me. I don't want to be stuck out on the road all night." She slumped beside the bike.

Neal stared into the night toward his home just a couple of miles away. Uneasiness swept over him. Something felt wrong. He didn't want to invite Dani to stay with them, but even with a pistol, it wouldn't be safe for her to camp along the road.

As he stared at the Harley and her, an idea formed. "There's a church a few miles from here. We're going that way. I'm sure you could stay there for the night and in the morning you can fix the Harley."

Dani stared at him for a moment as if trying to see deeper inside him. "Okay. It's been a long time since I was in a church." She struggled to stand the bike. "Lead the way."

"Do you want me to help you?" Neal asked.

"No. I can do this," Dani grunted and the bike rolled.

With a glance at her belly, Neal took Ginger's leash from Claire. Then he turned his gaze to Dani as she strained to roll the bike along. She could never push it up the hill.

For the next few minutes, they continued along the two-lane road, over a small stream and around a long curve. Progress seemed painfully slow. He remembered Beth saying that when things are frustrating, God is trying to teach patience.

Really, God? When I'm this close to home you want to teach me patience? He sighed.

Claire stared at him. "Is something wrong?"

"No." Neal planted a smile on his face.

"That's your creepy face grin again. Do you recognize this area?"

"Yes. Even in the dark."

Shouts and laughter broke the quiet of the night.

"This seems to be a night for yelling." Neal considered telling the women to wait while he checked out who the crazy person might be, but he figured that neither would stay behind.

As Ginger sniffed the air, Neal again passed the leash to Claire and then stepped around the curve.

The voice sounded happy and young. It also seemed familiar. He squinted, trying to see the person's face. He stepped from the forest and into the road, illuminated only by the crescent moon.

* * *

Night created more worries and increased the danger, but it also brought cool breezes that allowed Conner to pedal longer and faster toward Riverbank. He knew the way, but it all seemed different, even foreboding. Only an occasional flickering yellow light from a candle or campfire pierced the night. The black asphalt of a strip mall seemed endless with the large, tan, brick building beyond invisible. Unseen cows mooed in an unseen pasture.

"There it is!" Conner stopped his bike and ran to a street sign. "This is it!" He danced a jig several times around the pole. *Little brother, I'll be home in minutes.* "This is the sign for my street."

A few feet away, Madison laughed.

"Right up there, that's where it is, just up the hill."

Gravel crunched behind Conner. He spun around with his rifle ready.

A man holding a shotgun stepped out of the shadows. His clothes didn't fit well and he had the start of a salt and pepper beard, but his face looked strangely familiar.

"Dad?"

Fear and tension that had permeated Conner now gushed like a flood. His dad stood in front of him. He fought back the tears that welled in his eyes.

Neal slung the shotgun from his hands to a shoulder and stared. "Conner?"

"Yeah, it's me." He stepped close and they embraced. As Conner pressed against his dad, he knew that the long journey had ended and everything would be okay.

"I hardly recognized you." His father stepped back and looked him up and down. "I think we've both lost some weight."

"Where were you when the solar storm hit?" Conner asked.

"Near Grants Pass, Oregon." He shook his head. "I'm glad you were here."

Conner frowned.

Neal stared at Conner for a moment and then at the woman beside him.

She looked away.

"Conner … Where have you been?"

Torrents of guilt and anxiety flooded back upon Conner. "Remember our fight the night before you left?"

His father nodded.

In the distance, the rumble of motorcycle and truck engines disturbed the quiet.

A woman in a dark leather jacket pushing a Harley trudged from of the shadows. She glanced at the street sign and her eyes widened.

"You told me not to go hunting." Conner pursed his lips. "Well, I did."

"When did you get back?"

The Harley woman pushed her bike closer. "Ah … lovely family reunion and all, but figure it out later. You hear those vehicles? If the people driving them are who I think they are, we don't want them seeing us."

Conner nodded in agreement. "Let's get back to the farm. We can sort things out there."

The rumble of engines and vehicles grew.

"Okay." Neal waved at the others. "Let's head toward my farm." As they walked, he turned to Dani. "Who are these people following you?"

Conner gazed at the red Harley the woman pushed across the road. Then he spotted the satchel and goggles. "Your name is Dani?"

"Yeah." She smiled. "It's short for Danielle."

Madison stared at her. "The gang. They're looking for you."

The smile disappeared into an angry frown.

"And that's not your bike." Conner pointed. "Did you kill the man riding it?"

"What?" Neal looked from Conner to Dani.

"Let's explore my personal history later." With a grunt, Dani struggled to push her motorcycle off the road toward the woods. "We really need to get away from here."

Two motorcycles roared around the corner. One rider pointed toward the group and together they took cover in the trees just off the road.

"Dani, you can't get away," a man called.

"Go to the farm," Neal shouted at Conner and then darted into the bushes.

* * *

Only as Neal rushed behind bushes and bramble did he realize Claire had followed him. He gritted his teeth in frustration but remained otherwise silent for fear of revealing their position.

Dani lagged behind, pushing the Harley. As the others disappeared into the dark woods, Dani dropped the bike and darted after them.

Within seconds, a third bike and two pickups loaded with men arrived. The glare of headlights both hid and revealed. Neal struggled to count as armed men passed back and forth through light and into darkness, but felt certain more than ten had arrived and would soon be searching for Dani and anyone with her.

Two men walked in Neal's direction. He tensed, ready to shoot, but they collected Dani's bike and lugged it back to the trucks.

Neal allowed himself to breathe. He could have shot them, but what had they done to deserve it? Conner thought Dani had stolen the bike and perhaps killed the owner. Were these men just collecting what they owned? Probably not, but what did he know for sure? Perhaps these were thugs and she had fled from them. He needed answers.

Claire pointed to the nearby tree line. "Let's go," she mouthed.

Neal grunted agreement. Together they retreated into the forest and looked for the others. Neal led the way through the woods and then back to where the road wound up the hill. A ditch ran along one side, but the other shoulder made a gravel path with quick access to the forest if needed. Neal figured Conner might have the same idea or would at least follow the road.

Soon Neal heard twigs snap and hushed voices.

"The only thing I believe is that your name is Dani," Conner growled. "Why are they looking for you and how do we stop them?"

"Keep your voice down and keep moving," Dani whispered and turned away.

Conner grabbed her arm.

She spun around and pressed a pistol to his face. "Don't touch me."

Neal stepped into the grove with his shotgun pointed at Dani. "Put the gun down and start explaining."

"We need to hurry," Dani insisted but lowered her gun hand. "They won't stop looking for us."

Neal motioned for everyone to keep moving. "They seem to be after you. What would happen if they caught you?"

"Don't give me up to them." Dani shook her head. "That's not the solution."

"Why not?" Conner asked with an angry growl.

Dani opened the satchel and pulled out a large, neatly folded sheet of paper. "This is a map of Riverbank and the surrounding area. The Wolf Pack—"

"What?" Neal asked.

Dani shook her head. "They're the biggest gang south of Olympia, and besides killing and looting, they've been scouting the area."

Neal stared at the page but couldn't read it in the darkness. "Why would they be interested in Riverbank?"

"This town is the only one between Olympia and Longview that still has a working police force. The Wolf Pack doesn't like police and Roark, the alpha boss, wants to control the town."

"No, I don't believe you," Conner said flatly. "Why would you come here if the gang planned to attack?"

"I don't know this hick area!" Her face contorted in disgust. "When I travel this way I speed through on the freeway, but the pack blocked that route, so I tried the back roads. I've been turned around for most of the day." Dani cursed. "And I didn't know your place was right next to Riverbank. Just my lousy luck. Can we keep moving?"

"Yeah." Neal pointed. "We're near my farm. It's right—"

"I hear them." A man shouted in the darkness. "This way!"

"Get down." Neal pointed to a low spot nearby. "Stay quiet."

Twigs snapped and leaves crackled all around them.

Dani looked left and right into the darkness but remained standing.

"Hello, Dani. I'm glad we found you."

She dropped the satchel and took several steps toward the voice. "Why can't you just leave me alone?" she pleaded.

Neal froze. Why hadn't Dani fled or hid? He didn't want to leave her to an uncertain fate.

A flashlight clicked on, revealing a man with a goatee holding a pistol. "What kind of father would I be if I let you run off?"

"Father?" Neal looked at Dani and then at the man.

"My daughter has authority issues." The man grinned. "But what's a dad to do?" The grinned faded. "Take my daughter home."

Two men emerged from the darkness. She shouted curses and fought, but they dragged her away.

Roark pointed the pistol at Neal. "I don't like people messing with my family."

Another gang member stepped into the light. "Someone's coming. I heard movement and voices." He fired two shots into the darkness.

* * *

Evans Family Farm, Tuesday, September 13th

As sunlight turned to darkness, Drake lay on the couch, thinking of his parents. Even after all these years, he longed to see his mother again. Now his father had vanished and he ached to see him. Tears welled in his eyes and anger hardened his heart. Why had they left him?

He knew it was stupid, and wrong, to blame his mother for dying. But the pain of her going still lingered. Perhaps it always would.

Ashley walked into the room with a book and sat reading it.

He wiped his eyes and pretended to yawn.

Before his mother had died, his father rarely left Riverbank, but the last few years, conferences had become more important, more frequent. Drake felt his father's need to get away from the house—away from him. Conner had needed to get away too.

As Ashley read, Drake gazed at her long, blonde hair that draped over her shoulders and along her pink blouse. With each breath, her breasts rose and fell, gently stirring her curls.

She had been the sole bright spot in these recent terrible days. In her moment of need, she had thought of him ... ran to him. Unlike his father and brother, Ashley had stayed with him and helped him.

Deep down, he knew he would always protect her ... always want her.

He stood and stared at her glistening skin sparkling in the lamplight. His heart pounded in his ears.

She glanced up from her book and turned off the lamp. "It's getting dark. You should probably shut off the generator."

"Oh, yeah. I will." But he didn't move. "Would you ever leave here ... leave me?"

"If my parents return, I guess I'd have to go." Her gaze drifted down to the book. "But I want to stay here until then."

Drake trotted away with his thoughts still fixed on Ashley.

As he rolled the generator back into the garage, he heard the rumble of vehicles somewhere in the east. When he returned to the living room, Ashley had her face close to a side window.

She turned as he entered. "I thought I heard cars."

"I think you did." Drake found his night vision monocular, still on the tripod, and slung an AR-15 rifle over his shoulder. Then he grabbed an ammo can and stepped onto the porch.

Ashley followed with her shotgun and Gruff at her side.

Using the monocular, Drake scanned the area. "I don't see anything."

"Let's stay out here." Ashley settled onto the porch bench. "It's cooler."

Drake sat close and held her hand.

Gruff circled a couple of times and lay on the porch nearby.

"It's a nice night." Drake didn't really know what to say.

"Quiet. Peaceful." Ashley leaned against him. "Perfect."

What should he do next? Drake's mind raced for an awkward eternity. Should he put his arm around her? He wanted to kiss her, but should he just do it or say something meaningful about her first?

He decided to just do it and leaned close.

Gruff stood, looked toward the forest, and growled low.

Drake glanced at Gruff as he continued to growl, and then he heard it also, angry voices in the trees.

"Take Gruff in and lock the door." Drake grabbed the tripod, and with the rifle bobbing on his shoulder, darted to a small knoll near the house. Lying there, he would have good cover and remain nearly invisible. He set the tripod up beside a large alder and peered into the forest.

Two armed groups moved through the trees toward the farmhouse as if they knew exactly where they were going. Were they all bad guys?

Movement behind him caused Drake to turn.

Ashley plopped to her knees beside him.

"What are you doing out here?" Drake whispered.

"Gruff is in the house and the door is locked." She held the shotgun out for him to see. "And I'm trying to help."

A flashlight snapped on in the forest.

More angry voices shouted from the area where light shone in the darkness. Most were men, but there was definitely an angry woman shouting curses in the forest.

Two shots tore through the quiet.

Ashley fell to the ground with a scream.

Another shot boomed.

"Are you okay?" Drake could barely see her in the dark.

"Yeah, I think." She gulped air. "A bullet passed through my hair." Ashley brushed hands along her face and head. "I don't feel any pain or blood." She sighed.

Rage flared in Drake. He peered through the monocular and then fired the rifle.

Men fell, screamed, and ran as Drake poured rounds into the forest.

Click.

Drake slapped another magazine into the rifle and sprayed thirty more rounds on the shooters in the forest.

Click.

"Stop! Please stop!"

Drake hesitated. The voice from the darkness sounded familiar. He inserted another magazine and then peeked into the monocular.

A single arm waved from a nearby gully.

"You shot at my girlfriend." Drake's heart pounded with anger and adrenaline. "Leave or I'll kill all of you."

"No, we didn't shoot at you."

"Liar!" Drake took a deep breath. "Get out of here, now!"

"This is my home. Please stop shooting. My dad's been shot—"

"Conner?" Still holding his rifle, Drake stood as the word sank into him. "Dad? I shot Dad?" Drake ran into the darkness. He nearly tripped over one body and in the shadows of moonlight could see several more scattered on the forest floor. He looked right and left but didn't see his father.

Someone stood and ran to a body.

"Conner, is that you?" Drake asked.

"Yes," he said and cradled the head of a man lying face up on the ground.

Drake ran to his side. Even in the dim light, he recognized the faces of both his brother and father. A dark stain ran from the right side of his dad's chest.

"Noooo! I killed him! Killed my dad!"

Conner grabbed his brother by both arms and shook. "No. I saw what happened. You didn't do this."

Drake stared into his brother's eyes, wanting to believe him.

Ashley put her arm around Drake.

"A guy named Roark, the gang leader, shot Dad." Conner hugged him. "It happened just before you opened fire. I think you saved the rest of us."

A pregnant woman with a dog ran to them and clutched his father's hand. "He's alive. We need to get him inside. Where's your house?"

"This way." Ashley stood. "Follow me."

Conner and Drake lifted their father. Another woman about Conner's age helped and together they carried him home.

Gruff growled at the other dog, wagged his tail at Conner, Drake, and Ashley, and whined as they carried Neal to his bedroom.

"Can we get more light?" The pregnant woman glanced around the room. "I'll need medical supplies, bandages, antiseptic. Is there a doctor or hospital nearby?" She tore back the shirt, revealing a bloody entry wound on the right side.

"Drake, get the generator running and then go to Pastor Wayne." Ashley gestured in the direction of his house. "He should know how to find a doctor."

He nodded and ran from the room.

Ashley turned away but then stopped. "I'll get medical supplies from the survival closet, but we need at least one guard in case those guys come back."

"I will." Conner grabbed his rifle.

"I'll help you."

"Thanks, Madison." Leaving Claire to perform first aid, everyone else hurried from the room.

Day eleven

Evans Family Farm, Wednesday, September 14th

Drake awoke from a nightmare of gunfire, blood, and death to the faint light of dawn flowing through the living room window. He rubbed his eyes. The house seemed so quiet and peaceful. Had the horrible events of the past night been real?

As the last vestiges of sleep faded from his mind, Drake knew his brother had returned, and his father … how was his father doing?

A knock on the front door caused him to jump from the couch.

A bleary-eyed Ashley hurried in from the hallway with Gruff and Ginger following.

Conner appeared at the dining room entrance, holding a half-eaten apple.

Drake peered through the peephole. "It's Pastor Wayne." He opened the door and let him in.

"How's your father doing?" he asked, stepping in.

"Ah …." Guilt poured over Drake. He had fallen asleep and had no idea.

"Hanging on," Conner said as he walked across the room. "The doctor left with Deputy Campbell a few hours ago."

"They didn't move him to the hospital?" Pastor Wayne asked.

"All their fancy instruments were burned out by the sun storm." Conner frowned. "The doctor removed the bullet, cleaned and bandaged the wound. He'll be back later today, but … he's done about all he can."

"You make it sound like he's going to die." Drake shook his head and growled. "He's not."

Conner frowned but said nothing.

Madison hurried across the front lawn to the door. "I found the satchel."

"Let's sit in the dining room." Conner led the way.

The pastor sat next to Drake as Madison unfolded the map on the table.

Drake pointed. "Here's the lookout spot and the end of the fence just past our farm. Someone is definitely providing the gang with information about the defenses on the hill."

"Maybe, or it could be good recon. They're also interested in what the sheriff is doing in Riverbank." The pastor pointed to a spot on the map. "This is the police barricade on the freeway bridge."

Plodding steps from the hallway grabbed Drake's attention.

With red eyes and slumping shoulders, Claire entered the room. "Neal is stable. I gave him something to help him sleep. If he wakes, I think one or both of you guys should be with him."

"Can I get you something?" Madison asked.

"Tea, if you have any." She walked into the living room and collapsed on the couch.

"We do," Ashley said. "I'll get it. I know where things are." She hurried to the kitchen.

Conner stared at his brother for a moment and then returned his gaze to the map.

* * *

Several hours later, Drake entered his father's bedroom. Conner sat leaning back against the wall in a chair. His father lay on the bed, motionless and pale.

"How is he?" Drake asked.

"Still asleep, but I think the sedative is wearing off. He seems to be waking." Conner stood and stretched. "Call me if he does."

Drake nodded and stood there staring at his father. He had imagined his dad returning many times but not like this. He moved the chair and sat holding his father's hand. "We're okay, Dad. You just rest and get better."

Thinking that it might be good for his father to hear his voice, Drake told him everything that happened since the night of the solar storms. He started with a confession. "I wanted Conner to go hunting so I could have a party and when he left, I did. We really made a mess. I spent that first day after the storm cleaning the house." But along with the bad, there were things he wanted his father to know. "Ashley came the next day, really scared. I've been protecting her. I think you and Mom would be proud of me. But Dad, I've been really scared. I've shot and … I killed some people. I came close … real close, to shooting you."

His father moaned and his eyes fluttered open. "You didn't shoot me."

Drake gasped. "Everything's going to be okay, Dad." He ran to the door and threw it open. "Conner, Dad's awake."

Conner hurried in and leaned over the bed.

Tears rolled down Drake's cheeks.

Neal gazed at his boys and smiled. "Beth would be … is, so proud of both of you. I'm home. You're both here." He smiled. "I'm proud of you both."

Gradually his eyes closed, as if his father had gone to sleep.

Several minutes later, Drake leaned close. Tears ran down his cheeks. His father had died.

Day Twelve

Evans Family Farm, Thursday, September 15th

Before the sun had warmed the air the next morning, Pastor Wayne and several other men arrived at the Evan's farm. Conner spoke with them in the backyard and they began to dig.

Confused, Drake wandered out the back door. His father had died yesterday evening and his body still lay in the house. This was no time to be digging holes.

He froze midway across the yard. Conner and the others weren't digging a simple hole. This was his father's grave.

Tears rolled down his cheeks.

Conner hurried to him. "Go back inside. It's okay. We can do this."

More tears flowed. He retreated toward the house but then turned away. He didn't want anyone, especially Ashley, to see him like this. Tears were for boys and that time for him had passed.

Reaching the orchard, he wandered aimlessly through the trees. He stood there alone. *Why did you die? Why God—why did he have to go?*

When his mother had died, his father had retreated into this place. Hurt by her death, he had used the farm as a fortress against the world.

Drake marveled at the sudden insight but shook his head. He wouldn't withdraw from the community as his father had done. He had Ashley, Conner, Pastor Wayne, and others. Suddenly he wanted to, needed to, be with them. He ran back to the yard. Pastor Wayne stood by the grave with Ashley, Madison, Claire, and others.

The back door opened. Using careful steps, Conner and three other men exited the house, carrying a simple wooden litter. On it, wrapped in a white sheet, his father rested.

Drake hurried toward them. "I'll help carry Dad."

"You don't have to help." Conner shook his head.

Frustrated and a bit angry, Drake drew himself tall. "I'm not a baby. I've taken care of this farm since the sun storm. I can do this."

The slightest hint of a smile crossed Conner's face. He nodded. One of the men stepped aside and, across from Conner, Drake shared the burden of his father.

With Ashley on one side, Conner on the other, and friends all about, Drake watched as they lowered his father into the ground. He heard scattered words of the service only as interruptions of sorrow.

"The Lord promises us peace, not the peace of this world, but His peace," Pastor Wayne said.

Conner stood tall and straight, his face somber, like a marine at attention.

"Let not your heart be troubled and neither let it be afraid."

Claire sniffled.

"He is with us always ... until the end of the world."

Ashley wiped tears away. Drake felt certain that her thoughts were with her own parents.

After his father's body lay in the earth, people flowed back toward the house, but Drake stood staring at the grave, remembering the good times with his parents. Gradually, his gaze lifted. Ashley stood beside him, her eyes red and puffy.

His gaze drifted from her to the house, then to the barn and the garden beside it. Beyond that was the orchard of apple, pear, cherry, and plum trees. His father had built and equipped the farm to serve and protect his family. Now, he and Ashley would eat from the bounty. *Thanks, Dad.*

The door opened and Conner walked onto the porch. "When you're ready, there are a lot of people who would like to talk with both of you."

Holding Ashley's hand, Drake walked toward the house, confident that together they could face the storms to come.

Also by the Author

***Through Many Fires* (Strengthen What Remains, Book 1)** Terrorists smuggle a nuclear bomb into Washington, DC, and detonate it during the State of the Union address. Army veteran and congressional staffer Caden Westmore is in nearby Bethesda, Maryland, and watches as a mushroom cloud grows over the capital. The next day, as he drives away from the still burning city, he learns that another city has been destroyed, and then another. America is under siege.

* * *

***A Time to Endure* (Strengthen What Remains book 2)**

The exciting saga of Major Caden Westmore continues in this, the second book of the *Strengthen What Remains* series. In the first book, *Through Many Fires*, terrorists use nuclear bombs to destroy six American cities. Now, the nation's economy teeters on the verge of collapse. The dollar plunges, inflation runs rampant, and the next civil war threatens to decimate the wounded country. In the face of tyranny, panic, and growing hunger, Caden struggles to keep his family and town together. But how can he save his community when the nation is collapsing around it?

* * *

Braving the Storms **(Strengthen What Remains book 3)** In the third book of the series, a new and even more lethal problem emerges. A swift and deadly flu epidemic sweeps out of overcrowded FEMA camps and strikes the nation with horrific results. Caden Westmore struggles to keep his family and community safe, while others use the plague to advance their own military and political agendas. Caden must succeed, but how can he, when both the epidemic and chaos attack his hometown and family? .

About the Author

Hello, and thank you for reading.

I grew up in the mountains of Colorado and attended Mesa State College in Grand Junction. When money for college ran low, I enlisted in the United States Navy. I thought I would do four years and then use my veteran's benefits to go back to college. Life often doesn't go as we plan it.

While serving in the navy, I wrote space opera and military science fiction stories. Both ***Titan Encounter*** and the ***Final Duty*** stories fall into that period.

My first assignment was with a United States Navy unit at the Royal Air Force base in Edzell, Scotland. Two years later, while on leave in Israel, I met Lorraine from Plymouth, Devon, England. We married the next year. Together we spent the remainder of my twenty-year naval career traveling across the United States from Virginia to Hawaii and on to Guam, Japan, and beyond.

After I retired from the military, I taught in an Alaskan Eskimo village for several years while continuing to write. My first post-apocalyptic novel, ***Through Many Fires***, became an instant hit, rocketing onto the Kindle Science Fiction Post-Apocalyptic list and eventually making it to the number one spot. The second book in the series, ***A Time to Endure***, appeared on several genre bestseller lists and led to the recently released third book in the series, ***Braving the Storms***.

Today, Lorraine and I live on a small farm in Western Washington state. You can learn more about me on my website, kylepratt.me.

If you like this story

I am an independent writer, so I don't have an advertising budget. If you've read one of my books and found it entertaining, please tell your friends. Also, the more favorable reviews a book has, the better it sells. So if you liked the story, please consider writing a review on the site where you downloaded this ebook. If you don't like the story, please tell me why.

About the newsletter

Once a month I send out an email newsletter about upcoming books, events, specials, giveaways, promotions, and more—and I give a free ebook just for signing up! Use the link below. I respect your privacy and will never rent, sell, or give away your personal information.

Subscribe to the newsletter at: kylepratt.me/contact/

Made in the USA
Las Vegas, NV
19 November 2021